Death Will Have Your Eyes

Also by James Sallis

FICTION

A Few Last Words (1970)
The Long-Legged Fly (1992)
Moth (1993)
Black Hornet (1994)
Limits of the Sensible World (1994)
Renderings (1995)

NONFICTION

The Guitar Players (1982, 1994)
Difficult Lives (1993)

AS EDITOR

The Shores Beneath (1971)
The War Book (1972)
Jazz Guitars (1984)
The Guitar in Jazz (1996)
Ash of Stars: On the Writing of Samuel R. Delany (1996)

AS TRANSLATOR

Saint Glinglin by Raymond Queneau (1993)

Death Will Have Your Eyes

A Novel about Spies

James Sallis

St. Martin's Press

New York

DEATH WILL HAVE YOUR EYES. Copyright © 1997 by James Sallis.
All rights reserved. Printed in the United States of America. No part
of this book may be used or reproduced in any manner whatsoever
without written permission except in the case of brief quotations
embodied in critical articles or reviews. For information, address
St. Martin's Press, 175 Fifth Avenue, New York, N.Y. 10010.

Design by Ellen R. Sasahara
Edited by Gordon Van Gelder

Library of Congress Cataloging-in-Publication Data
Sallis, James.
    Death will have your eyes / James Sallis.—1st ed.
        p.   cm.
    ISBN 0-312-15513-1 (hardcover)
    I. Title.
    PS3569.A462D43   1997
    813'.54—dc21   97-9165
                                                    CIP

First edition: July 1997

10 9 8 7 6 5 4 3 2 1

To Adrian and Clif

Verrà la morte e avrà i tuoi occhi.

Death will come,
and will have your eyes.

—CESARE PAVESE

1

THE MAN KEPT opening his mouth, wanting something
from me, but it was a language I didn't know. Not Man-
darin. Not Thai or Vietnamese. Only sounds. His voice
rose and fell in pitch. Shouting, demanding. I shook my
head, the sour, foul smell of my own body washing up
over me in waves, tongue so swollen I could not talk,
could not respond. Soon the pain would start again. And
I would rise, hover near the ceiling looking down.
Watching. Apart.

I woke suddenly, rushing to exchange the currency
of dreams for coin I could spend. Morning light fell daz-
zlingly through the skylight onto the futon. Those wide
shadows were not bars or slats in a cage—only the leaves
of plants in hanging baskets up there. That sound was
only the phone.

Nothing else in the room. No windows. The futon,
a painted bamboo screen against one wall, an expanse of
blond wood floor—tongue and groove I'd put in myself. About as close as the real world gets to the ordered
simplicity of oriental drawings.

No one else, either. Only Gabrielle and myself.

She slept crosswise on the futon, my head cradled in her lap. Trying to get away from the light, I turned over. "Oh yes, *please*," she said. But obviously the phone was not going to quit ringing, so I snaked along the bed to answer it. Gabrielle grabbed me as I went by and held on.

I listened for a moment and hung up. "Wrong number," I told her. "*I've* got your number," she said, head moving to replace her hand, but I stopped her, wrapping black hair around both my hands and pulling her up into a slow, easy kiss.

"I'm going for a run," I said. "Get the sludge out. Want to come along?"

"At *six* in the bleedin' *mornin'*?"

With Gabby you never knew what accent you might get. Her features came mostly from an Irish mother and patrician Mexican father, but her extended family was pure goulash. Dad left when she was three, and she and her mother spent years shuttling from household to household, family to family, country to country. This early morning, the accent was British, a better choice than most, I suppose, for gradations of polite outrage.

"Okay, but don't say I didn't ask. So go back to sleep now, my little peasant."

"Pheasant?"

"Peasant. Half an hour, tops, even with a head wind. I'll bring breakfast."

"And here I thought you *were* breakfast."

"Miss, have you considered taking up a hobby?"

"No time for it."

"That was my point."

She shrugged. "One stays with what one's good at.

Run along now," she said, and was asleep again before I got shorts and shoes on.

I stood watching her a moment—her compact brown body against light blue sheets, breasts just a little too heavy, rib cage set high—then went into the bathroom. Turned on the radio there. It was Mozart, a serenade performed on "original" instruments which the musicians wrestled valiantly to bring into tune. Thousands upon thousands of dollars, thousands upon thousands of hours, had been expended on this bogus authenticity, these elaborate counterfeits. I washed my face and brushed my teeth, then stood at the window looking out till the piece was over. One doesn't hang up on Mozart.

There were few others in the park that early: a handful of runners and dog walkers; one young mother who looked remarkably like Shirley Temple pushing a pram; another trotting along with three children at her heels, all of them androgynous looking and none over five years old; street people starting off on their day's boundless odyssey. Birds and squirrels worried at yesterday's leavings, perhaps hoping their investigations would help them understand these huge, dangerous beings that lived in their midst.

I swung around the park's perimeter in an easy jog, following an asphalt bike path, and stopped at a pay phone on the far side, the kind of old-fashioned booth you rarely see anymore. There I dialed a number I still knew all too well. It was picked up on the first ring.

"Age has slowed you, perhaps."

"As you must realize, I was in no hurry to return this call. At first, I was not even sure that I wanted to respond at all. And after eight years—"

"Actually, it just slipped over the edge into nine."

"—I believed it likely that whatever business you think you have with me could wait a few more minutes."

"Perhaps. However, your plane departs at ten or thereabouts. American, Flight eight seventeen. You are Dr. John Collins, a dentist on vacation."

"Sir."

Silence.

"It has been, as you say, nine years. I have a career, a new life, commitments."

Silence still.

"I am no longer in your employ."

A still longer silence. Then finally: "It will be good to see you again, David."

I hung up and ran back the way I'd come, pushing myself now. A light breeze was coming up, and full sunlight struck the artificial lake at a slant, tossing off sheets of glare. Birds and squirrels didn't seem any closer to understanding us. Neither did I.

They were waiting by the benches about halfway around, in a space partially screened by trees. You wouldn't be able to see much, here, either from the street or adjacent apartments. So some thought had gone into it, at least.

One was in jeans, black sweatshirt and British Knights, twentyish, a broad, pale-complected man with bad skin. His head kept tic-ing convulsively towards his right shoulder, crossing and recrossing the same minute, almost imperceptible arc. The other was maybe ten years older, wearing what had once been an expensive suit, with a chambray dress shirt frayed to white at the cuff and loose threads at the collar, and a knit tie with the knot tugged down to his breastbone. Lank brown hair tucked behind his ears.

"Your money, sir?" the younger one said, stepping in front of me. "Don't mean to hurt you. This can all be over with in half a minute, you want."

Chest heaving, heart throwing itself again and again against rib cage, I sank onto one of the benches. A placard alongside documented this as STATION NINE (9). Pictographs indicated that I was to restretch muscles and tendons, check my pulse against my own personal MHR, perform ten to twenty deep knee bends.

". . . Minute," I said. Then, catching my breath: "I don't carry money when I'm running, boys. Better pick another pigeon."

"Done *got* our pigeon." The older one. He raked straying hair behind one ear with the open fingers of his hand. Ran his nose quickly along that coat sleeve. It was slick already from prior crossings. "Just got to fry it up now. Drumsticks."

I glanced briefly at him, and when I did, the younger one made his move.

With amateurs, it's always easier when there's more than one. Then you can use them effectively against each other, the same way you use an attacker's own momentum against him in classic judo. That's the physical part. But they also get overconfident: safety in numbers and all that. And even those who know something about what they're doing can get sloppy or, hesitating to check on the other one, let down their guard for that essential brief second.

With these guys I swiveled into a basic high-low, unwinding like a spring, low and moving inexorably right-

· 5 ·

ward to take out the younger one with a sideways blow to the knee as I spun past, then on past the older one, coming in high and behind as he was looking down to see what happened to his partner, watching him crumple from an open-handed blow just below the third cervical vertebra as I went past.

I followed the arc out to its natural stop and straightened, concerned. You never lose the reflexes, but the edge fades on you. You lose the exact touch, where imperceptible gradations can mean the difference between stunning an adversary and permanently damaging him. I was afraid I might have come down a little too hard.

But apparently not. If anything, from my concern over going in too hard and fast—when I shouldn't have been thinking at all, simply reacting—I'd held back. The older guy had already climbed to his feet and was staggering towards me with a hunting knife he'd tugged out of his boot.

I felt all consciousness of self melt away, felt myself dissolving into motion, reflex, reaction.

The knife clattered onto cement and he lay in a grassy patch beside a bench, elbow shattered, face draining of color.

"Please," he said. "Oh shit. *Please.*"

I stood there a moment. Yesterday, even an hour ago, what had just happened would not have. I'd have handed over whatever money I had, talked to them. Or simply run. And yesterday, even an hour ago, once it *had* happened, I would have called the police and awaited them. I'd spent years trying to turn myself off, shut the systems down, before I was finally successful. And now the switch had been thrown again: deep within myself, whether or not I wished it, whether or not I accepted it, I was again active, and on standing orders.

So I left the muggers there, knowing they were people with complicated histories and frustrated needs like my own and probably didn't deserve what had happened to them, and went home to Gabrielle.

She stumbled into the kitchen just as I was finishing breakfast, wearing one of my T-shirts, which hit her midthigh, and white socks that had started off at the knee and now were bulky anklets. She took the cup of tea I handed her, looked at my face and said, "What's wrong, Dave? Something has happened."

"Sit down." I slid a plate of buttered rye toast, fruit and cheese in front of her. Ceramic plate, thrown on a wheel near Tucson, signed by the artist, all brilliant blues and deep greens. I sat opposite her with my own tea, in a mug from the same set.

"This is going to be difficult."

"Yeah, looks that way. But we've been through a lot together. And we've always handled it."

"Nothing like this, G, believe me."

I looked at the window, wondering how the birds and squirrels were doing, then at her face. So familiar, so filled with meaning for me. So open to me now.

"Everything you know about me, everything you think you know, is false."

"No," she said.

"Yes. I have to tell you that much, have to insist on it. But for good reason I can't tell you more, not now. Now I have to ask you to do something for me, to do it immediately and without question."

After a moment she nodded.

"I want you to pack whatever you absolutely must have and I want you to go away. Not back to your apartment, but somewhere—anywhere—else. Preferably out of the city. I don't want to know where you are. In a week, a month, whenever I can, *if* I can, I'll come and find you."

"It would be easier if I knew why, Dave."

"Yes. It would."

"But I don't *have* to know."

She was away maybe ten minutes and came back into the kitchen with a huge over-the-shoulder bag and one small suitcase. I sat at the table and drank my tea, looked out the window. Heard sirens nearby, then, as though just an echo, others far away. Watched an ambulance pull up at a brownstone down the street, lights sweeping.

"Well," she said.

"You're an extraordinary woman, Gabrielle. I love you, you know."

"Yes. You do."

And she was gone.

Outside, several million lives went on as though nothing had happened.

After a while I walked through the archway into the studio. Began capping tubes and cans of paint, turning off burners and hot plates under pots of wax, soft metals, glue. It would be a long time before I came back here, if I came back at all.

At one end of the long room, by the windows, sat the piece I'd been working on, a forbidding mass of mixed materials—burlap, clay, metals, wood, paper—from which a shape struggled to release itself. You could feel the physicality, the sheer exertion, the intensity, of that struggle. I threw a tarp over it and as the tarp descended, the sculpture's form, what I'd been seeking, what I'd been trying to uncover for so long, came to me all at once: suddenly I could see it.

2

Awake in a motel room at two in the morning, thinking of Gabrielle.

I'd flown straight through to St. Louis, then by connecting flight to Memphis, where at debarkation a message, and this room, awaited Dr. Collins. Ate dinner, something called a "patty melt" held in place on the plate by barricades of french fries smelling of fish, at a Denny's two blocks away, since there was nothing else close by; came back to the room with a Styrofoam cup of coffee and watched half a cable movie about a Pole who'd shoehorned his way into the KGB. Then I pulled a book out of my bag but, distracted by memory as much as by the present, finally gave that up as well.

My room was on the second floor, with a sweeping view of the approach: parking lot, street, strip of bars and second-string businesses opposite. The motel itself backed up flush against another building. Once (and still, I supposed) we had hundreds of such safe rooms spread about the continental U.S. and most of Western Europe. Its stairs were cement and steel. They rumbled like distant thunder or a muted percussion section, bass drums, kettles, gongs, whenever someone mounted them.

At this hour only an occasional truck passed outside, but the smell of auto exhaust lingered, so many olfactory ghosts. Behind that, a verdant smell, compounded of pecan and magnolia trees, stretches of bright green grass, honeysuckle, mildew, mold: Delta land was rich land. Still farther back, at some level, sensory awareness of the river itself. The bottom two inches of my window were permanently ajar, the aluminum frame immovable. Smells, sound and moonlight spilled over its rim into my room. Including, once, the hoot of an owl adrift in this city at the border of its homeland.

For many years, longer than I wanted to think about, I had lived on the edge, at the verge. I was good at what I did: fast when fast was needed, slow when that seemed to promise better results, always efficient, often surprising in my solutions both to the original problem and those inevitably developing from it. But then one day in Salvador as I stood watching a red Fiat burn, I realized that it was over for me—as though I'd stepped through an unseen door, looked up and found the world transformed in ways I could not fathom, or had blundered over borders into a foreign country where familiar words meant inexplicable things.

Not that I stopped believing in what I was doing. I'm not sure I *ever* believed in what I was doing; it was simply what I did, what I was programmed to do, the way I defined myself and negotiated my days. But it occurred to me there in Salvador that I was becoming what I did—that there was little else, little more, to me. And once I'd paused, even for that moment, I could never get back in step, never remember how the centipede walked.

So I climbed down off the edge I'd blunted with others' blood and my own.

And I'd spent the past nine years turning myself into a human being. Learning to care, to feel, to trust, to let go. At first it had been all form, just going through the motions, and I often felt like some alien creature painstakingly learning to pass, to give a good imitation of humanity. But in time, as it will, form became content.

Now I was reentering the old life—briefly, true, but already it began to feel familiar—and in many ways it was as though that nine years had never been. Except . . .

Except that Gabrielle had been a big part of my transformation. Except that I carried Gabrielle, carried my feelings for her and memories of our years together, within me now, and always would. Maybe none of us finally is anything more than the residue of those he's known and loved.

Blaise's cratered face came back to me: "You must not *think*. Cast away everything, David, let it go, let your *spine* become brain. The body has an intelligence of its own, far older than your mind's."

Blaise had trained me, trained us all. Taught us to stay alive. And if ever I had loved anyone in that prior life, I had loved him. Leaving the agency, leaving that life, I felt that I had to leave Blaise as well: one of the few regrets I allowed myself, but it was a profound one.

In my years as a soldier (for that's what we always called ourselves, among ourselves) I lived without personal identity, slipping in and out of roles and temporary lives as easily, and as readily, as others change clothing. I had been many people, known many people, taken part in many dramas and not a few (albeit unintentional) comedies. One thing I knew absolutely was that the stories we live by are as real as anything else is. As long as we do live by them. Even when we *know* they're lies.

Towards morning I dreamed that Gabrielle was above me, moving steadily upon me, head thrown back and black hair catching light from the window. Then something changed and my hands, reaching up, touched not flesh, but canvas, steel, the rough grain of wood. I opened my eyes again in the dark and saw it there over me. Half-formed, unalive, its weight ever increasing, it continued to move upon me: the sculpture I'd left behind, unfinished, at the studio.

3

Towards dawn another thing happened as well.

The old training, the reflexes, were flooding back all at once, and I don't know what cue alerted me, some minutely perceptible shift in the volume of sound outside, a muted footfall or mere sense of presence, but I was awake, *waiting* for the sound, before the sound came.

The sound was my door being tried.

There was a pause, a silence, then the lisp of a flexible pick entering the door lock. Senses at full alert, I could almost feel the tension as again the knob was turned hard right, till it stopped, and held there. The pick raked its way slowly, methodically, along the lock's pin-tumblers.

It had happened a few times before when I was concentrating like this, and it happened now: I was outside *my* self, in another self. I watched my hands (except they weren't mine) working at the lock, felt a trickle of sweat down the middle of my back, became aware of the weight of a folded paper in the side pocket of my coat.

For a moment it rippled back from there. I sat in a large rented room off a hall so narrow that people had to turn sideways to pass one another. The room smelled of canned meats and beef stew, stale coffee, the bathroom four doors away. Bedroom and living room furniture were jumbled together indiscriminately. A stack of newspapers squatted under a low window looking out onto a wall, with a sliver of morning light showing at the top.

Then the ripples spread. I was nineteen and terrified, running beneath a thick canopy of green. Minutes ago there had been a riot of birdsong; now the only sounds were my boots slapping into puddles and sucking their way back out, the staccato gabble of those pursuing me in the distance, my own thudding heart.

And, again, my heart pounding: but now when I reached out, my hand fell not against vines and undergrowth, but onto the waist of a slim, dark woman in white shorts and sandals. She stirred in her sleep.

Then, like a thread suddenly unraveling, giving way, it was all gone. I was back in my own body and mind. Back with the old training, the old reflexes.

By the time he got the door unlocked, I was out of bed and in a dark juncture of shelf and wall. By the time he crossed to the bed, pausing twice to listen closely, I was aping his own footsteps. And by the time he realized no one was there, and turned, I was behind him.

"The weather tomorrow will be fair," I said, "with temperatures in the mid-60s and a light southeasterly wind, brisker towards evening."

He started to speak, then simply shook his head. He was thirtyish, with flat gray eyes, blond hair, a tan poplin suit. He wasn't new at this. He'd been at one end or another of it many times before.

"It would be terrible to miss such a day," I said. "We have so few of them."

A lengthy silence as his eyes caught my own, and held. Then: "The seasons do go on."

"Yes," I said.

Another long silence.

"I do not know you."

I shook my head. "Nor I, you. It can stay that way."

"Yes. Sometimes that is the best choice." He looked briefly about the room. "It seems the client neglected to provide me with information necessary to executing the assignment."

"There's not a lot of professionalism left."

"He failed to tell me what you were. I would have to say that such bad faith voids the contract. You would agree?"

"I would." But this man's utter humorlessness, those gray eyes round and flat and hard as lentils, still frightened me.

"Good," he said. He watched light sweep quickly along the wall, snag in a corner and momentarily brighten there, then fade, as a car passed outside. "I was to kill you, you know."

I nodded.

"Would I have been able to do that?" He remained staring at the wall, as though awaiting the next car.

I held out a hand, palm up. "You didn't." And shrugged. "Maybe the only things that *can* be, are those that *are*."

"But we will never know." Philosophy at five in the morning with the man who came to take you down: we lead a rich life, out here on the edge.

He looked back at me.

"Only once before have I come to kill a man and turned away from it."

"Then I'm glad I could be here to share this moment with you."

After a moment he said: "A joke."

I nodded.

He nodded back. "I was sixteen. I went into my father's room, where he was, as most nights, drunk and sleeping. I had brought along a knife from the kitchen, the sharpest one I could find. For a long time I stood with the knife poised above his chest, looking down at him, slowly coming to understand that I did not have to kill him now, that it was enough just to know how easily I could have. That was the last time I saw him."

He still had not moved. His eyes remained on mine.

"His grave is covered with kudzu now. You know about kudzu? Amazing stuff. Brought over from Japan to help control erosion, then it started taking over everything. Climbs radio towers, covers entire hills a foot or two deep. People have to go out every day and chop it back from their yards."

Lights again went by outside, but barely showed on the wall. He started towards the door and I went along.

"The man you will be wanting to see is Howard the Horse. He will not be wanting to see you."

"And where would I start looking?"

"You would probably start looking at a greasy spoon on Ervay and North Main." He pronounced it *greezy*. "You would probably stop looking there, too."

"A joke."

Nothing. Not a blink, not even a shrug.

"Mindy's Diner. Corner table, rear. Guy wears a jockey cap year 'round, day and night. Looks to be the same cap going on ten years now."

"Thanks."

"Think of it as professional courtesy."

"I owe you."

"No. No one owes me."

We walked to the door together. I opened it for him.

"Enjoy the fine weather tomorrow," I said.

He looked back. After a moment he said, "You too."

4

MACARONI CHEESE
RED BEENS & RICE
MUSTARD GREENS COOKED WITH SALT PORK

BEETS
MASH POTATOS
GREEN BEENS (CHOOSE TWO)

THE BLACKBOARD HUNG on a side wall, eraser dangling from it by a foot or so of heavy string, menu chalked on in scraggly printed letters.

Those of us who are close to forty, our fathers used to take us to places like Mindy's on rare nights mom was at work or for some other reason not home. That was back before fast-food spots sprang up four to every street corner; going in there reminded me how much things have changed, and how little we notice it.

There were two or three career coffee drinkers art-fully arranged at the counter, lime-green Formica printed with those sketchy boomerang shapes you saw every-where in the fifties; a couple of kids sitting together in a booth sopping up grease out of waxed-paper wrappers with their hamburgers; a scatter of older folk with one or another of the day's $4.95 specials, drink and roll included.

I could just make out a steamy corner of the kitchen through the gunport-like window behind the counter. From time to time heads ducked down to peer out, or disembodied hands and arms slid out plates heaped with food. At least two radios were playing back there.

Howard the Horse was, indeed, at his accustomed table, jockey cap everything I'd been led to expect. I was reasonably sure it had started out yellow. Howard himself had started out lanky, gaunt. Ichabod Crane was still in there somewhere, sunk in Nero Wolfe's body, waiting. As I approached, he tore open two packets of sugar and dumped them into a glass of milk. Then he slowly drank it all, watching me over the rim of the glass as I sat across from him. The sugar had turned to sludge at the bottom. He kept the glass tilted till the sludge had snailed down the side into his mouth. Then he put the glass on the table with his hand still on it and watched me some more.

"How old are you?" he said.

I told him.

He snorted. A little milk came out of one nostril.

"Young." Though I wasn't.

He shook his head and dabbed at the milk, almost daintily, with a shirt sleeve. "Used to be young myself. Long ago, in a land far away: you know? I can almost remember it, sometimes. Now I got your basic sugar diabetes, your basic ulcers, your basic high blood. Bad hearts in my family, on both sides, as far back as anyone can remember. When it rains, I can't breathe. When it's dry, I can't breathe. Few days I *can* breathe, my ankles start swelling up like snakebites." He pushed the glass away. "So what can I do for you?"

"Sounds like I better ask fast, before you keel over on me."

"Maybe you should at that, boy. Not the kind for keeling over, though. Most likely just stay propped up here and looking pretty much like I always do. Could even be some time before anyone noticed a difference, come to think of it."

He held up a hand. The waitress must have been watching for his sign and poured him another glass from a plastic jug under the counter. She brought it over and asked if I wanted anything. I thanked her and said no. He reached for two more sugars.

"So you don't want food or a cup of coffee, what *do* you want?"

"I have trouble sleeping."

"I remember that too, being able to sleep. Almost as good as eating whatever you want. Sleep till noon, pull the covers up over your head and sleep till it started getting dark again. Now I know every crack in my ceiling like I know my shoe size. But a man your age, there's no excuse for *you* having trouble like that. Get yourself a woman, son. Or a hot bath. A bottle."

"Whatever works."

"You got it. Good old all-American pragmatism."

"I think the reason I can't sleep is because I have this dream there's someone in the room with me, Howard."

He didn't say anything, but he knew. He dumped in his sugars, drank his milk.

"In voodoo lore," I went on, "spirits take over the bodies of mortal men, inhabit them and use them to their own purposes. Those bodies are called their horses. Is that why they call *you* Horse, Howard?"

He put the empty glass down. "You're the one calling himself Collins."

I nodded.

Problems were developing between supply and demand. Several times the waitress, a wiry redhead somewhere between thirty and fifty, wearing pressed jeans and a *Who? Me?* sweatshirt, had shouted back into the kitchen following up on orders and been ignored. Now she picked up a dirty plate from the counter and sailed it frisbeelike through the window. It broke against the wall with a hollow snap.

" 'M I gonna have to come back there like I did last week? Huh? You boys want t' talk about each other's mothers or take knives to each other, I could care less, but you better do it on your own damn time, you hear me?"

Two streams of rapid-fire Spanish from the kitchen: suggestions as physiologically incorrect as they were politically so.

"Yeah, whatever. Could be fun," the waitress said. "But right now, either I see my orders on this window in two minutes or you're both out of here. *Comprende,* gentlemen? And shut off that music."

The music didn't get shut off, but it did get turned down. Two or three plates of food thumped onto the ledge.

"Has a real way with words, Linda has," Howard said. "Charm the buzz off a bee."

He turned back to me.

"I'm a postman, nothing more," he said. "You do understand that?"

"I can accept it. And rain or shine is up to you, postman. I'll have to ask for a return address."

"I can give you a name. I don't know how much good it'll do you," he told me. "Think you might get me another glass of milk before you leave? I usually limit myself to two, but—" With a quick dip of head and hand he shooed away whatever might have followed that *but*.

I went over to the counter, brought the milk back to him, set it down. He sat holding glass and sugar packets, nodding his thanks.

"I been doing this a long time," he said. "I know a few people, people around a long time like me, and I talked to some of them."

I waited.

"You been away a while. My friends knew you. But these boys that wanted the package mailed, they're kind of new hands at all this. Guess they must of thought you were too."

"But you went ahead and sent your man around anyway."

He shrugged. "How else these boys gonna learn? No one teaches 'em anything anymore. Don't be too hard on 'em."

He poured in sugar.

"Besides, like I told you: I'm just a postman."

He drank, waited for the sludge, put the glass down and thanked me again.

"Take care," he said. "There aren't many of us left."

No one knows why the dinosaurs vanished. With our kind, it's a lot simpler.

5

In the cabin window, against the city's pinpoint lights, what Neruda called "the diminutive fires of the planet," I saw: a man in his forties rushing headlong from everything that had sustained him, rushing towards the things that almost destroyed him. But within those things, in large part, were the seeds of what he'd become, what he was, what he couldn't (however he tried) leave behind.

Following my designated assassin's departure, I'd gone back to bed, later had a leisurely midmorning breakfast, then in early afternoon paid my visit to Harry. Two hours still remained before my flight, and I had passed them in a bar by the departure gate drinking Perrier. The same people were milling around who'd been milling around years ago when I spent a lot of time in airports.

I was on my way to Dallas. The message left for me in Memphis had directed me there, to DayRest Motel in Oak Cliff where, as I sank slowly through southwestern skies, I would become Jorge Sanchez and (the message had no need to tell me this part) await further instructions. The address that Howard the Horse gave me also belonged to Dallas.

Just before takeoff a young woman had slipped into the seat beside me, and we spent much of the early part of the flight talking. She was twenty-six, Indian, traveling from New York City, where she lived and worked as a CPA, to attend her husband's graduation from engineering school at SMU. It was an arranged marriage; married a year, they had spent one long initial week and six evenly spaced weekends together. She kept telling me how nervous she was. Now, after a few pages of something gargantuan by Michener and a brief plunge into what appeared to be a prayer or inspirational book of some kind, she'd fallen asleep. Cities scrolled by below us.

And I was thinking about Gabrielle again.

I'd been alone a long time. For a year or more after quitting, I sat in my rented room and read things I'd always wanted to read and a lot of other things I'd never even known existed. I ate in anonymous lunchrooms and delis, usually with a book propped before me, and talked to almost no one. I walked in the streets and parks for hours at a time, watching people closely, all the different ways they linked themselves or kept apart. And I spent whole days in galleries and museums, slowly coming to realize that my future, whatever future I had, was bound up with these places, with what they stood for. At one point, I remember, every wall of my room was papered with prints and reproductions torn from books bought cheaply in secondhand stores near the college: Cézanne, Delvaux, Redon, Renoir, Dalí, Rothko, all of it in a dazzling, undifferentiated jumble. This was some time before my first makeshift studio and longer still before my first real piece, but studio and piece were there already, nascent, in the half-life I was living. A future had begun coalescing even as I moved blindly (and trying to learn to see) towards it, and in one of the museums on a dim, low November day, I met Gabrielle.

She worked there as a part-time guide, just as she worked as a substitute teacher, as an occasional waitress, as a spear carrier for the opera, as a ballet or tennis tutor. All were ways of staying safely out of the mainstream, of remaining (she liked to say) at the center of her own life and (she'd add, laughing) not ever getting *too* bored.

A major Matisse show was in progress, and Matisse, the way he repealed not just perspective but depth itself, the way he handled large forms and pools of pure color, had recently become important to me. I wound up sitting much of the afternoon in a room full of work from the *Jazz* period. Individuals straggled through. A guard circulated erratically. Tour groups eddied in and out. Then just after the museum's closing was announced, someone came and sat beside me.

"You really like these, don't you?"

I nodded and looked at her.

"Especially these two." She pointed. I nodded. She pointed again. "I couldn't help noticing. When I came through with my tours." She held out her hand. "My name's Gabrielle. Tell me: do you usually have dinner after a tough day of museum-going?"

"Usually."

"Early, I bet."

"Early."

"And alone?"

"Almost always."

"But not tonight."

"I hope not." We stood and walked together towards the door. "My name's David," I told her.

"Come with Gabrielle, David."

Late that night I had returned to a cozy, safe room suddenly gone bare and cold. I stood for what seemed hours looking out at a blood-red moon, at trucks being loaded from the docks across the street for early-morning hauls. I was thinking that I'd just received, without warning, fanfare or expectation, an invitation to rejoin the human race, RSVP. Towards dawn I picked up Pavese.

6

Two days later I was sitting in Johnsson's office saying, "No, sir."

It was not something he was used to hearing. He dealt with it by waiting to see if I was through, then, when I added nothing more, simply went on talking.

"No, sir," I said again, interrupting him, something he was even *less* used to. It's conceivable that no one had ever interrupted him before. "I will not pull down Luc Planchat for you. Or for anyone else."

He waited again. A bird on the window ledge outside peered fiercely in at us. I thought how birdlike Johnsson himself was. Heavy brow, dark recession of eyes, the stillness in them.

"Yet it appears," he said, "that this must be done."

"According to information you have received, yes. But in the first place, that information remains circumstantial. And secondly, since your own agency has no specific intelligence function, most of that information was piped in from another agency—"

He nodded.

"—one with which you have had disputes in the past—"

No nod this time.

"—and is therefore suspect."

"Perhaps so. One takes nothing at face value, of course."

"Including your own veracity in reporting this information to me."

"There is that, yes. Do you believe I would lie to you, David?"

"Freely. Outrageously. The good reporter looks at his scattered facts, then starts cobbling them into shoes that will fit. There's always an agenda: political, aesthetic, personal. Connect the dots. Constellations."

"You're right, of course. I would do whatever I thought necessary to get done what I thought must be. And so, in another time, would you have."

"It *was* another time, sir." After a moment I added: "If Planchat needs taking out, they should be the ones to do it."

"Ah: *should*. A most dangerous word."

He moved for the first time since we'd begun talking, taking his hands from the chair arms and folding long fingers together on his lap. I thought again of the feet of predatory birds. There was no desk in the room, only chairs with various tables alongside, many of them antiques picked up at flea markets, estate and garage sales. Johnsson hated desks. Hated people who sat behind them. Hated cages.

"Removal, you understand, is no longer a part of their agency's charter."

"And it is of yours."

"As it has always been."

Something suspiciously like a smile darted across his face and was gone.

"They created Planchat," I said. "And then they decided—or someone decided, at whatever level—that the model was obsolete."

"Perhaps more an anachronism than obsolete: *their* thinking, of course, not my own. A killing machine, David. The finest, certainly the most artful, ever devised."

"Yes. And if the machine needs unplugging, it's their responsibility."

"Absolutely. No one would argue that. It *is* their responsibility. But it's also our job: what we do."

"It's not what *I* do, sir."

He looked at me for several moments.

"Very well," he said. "I suppose it is possible that nine years can change a man, perhaps even past the point of recognition."

"Or in that time, the man can change himself."

"By his own bootstraps, yes. I understand that you're an artist now. Critics write of the 'contained violence' and gentleness of your—do you call them statues?"

"*Pieces,* usually. Or just *work.* Most of them aren't sculpture in any classical sense."

He nodded. Anyone not watching closely would have missed it.

"The word *poise* is often used. Meaning, I take it, a kind of rare and comely balance."

"By some."

"Of course: by some."

Neither of us spoke for a time then. Out on the ledge

the bird's audition continued. Darkening clouds nudged at the sky. Finally, as imperceptibly as, earlier, he had nodded, he shook his head.

"Be cautious about settling for memory, David. It's far too thin a gruel for the like of us to live on."

I said nothing.

"I suppose that you may have changed in fundamental ways, after all. And I cannot say, finally, that I am sorry for that. I suppose it's time for you to go back to your Gabrielle now, back to your work, your 'pieces.' Thank you for coming."

I stood and held out my hand. After a moment his own left his lap and falteringly searched mine out.

"Forgive me," he said. "I forget, and you could not have known. But for several years now I have been quite blind."

I told him that I was sorry, and to take care.

"David . . . ," he said when I was almost to the door. "A single favor."

"Yes, sir."

"An old friend has many times asked after you. Go and see him. It will not take you long."

"Blaise."

He nodded.

"You will find him here."

He held out a card. I walked back across the room and took it from him. His hand lingered there after it was gone.

7

Two days past, on a hillside in Oak Cliff, the motel-room TV won't work, bringing in only dim gray forms and phantoms behind a wash of dots, and the real world outside my window, awash with gray drizzle, is little more defined.

Jorge Sanchez lies on his bed in paint- and plaster-spattered jeans and sweatshirt waiting. Occasionally there is lightning far off, or a climb of car lights up the wall. The couple next door (possibly a threesome) has left off its lovemaking, and someone over there's drawing a bath now. The whining glide of a steel guitar reaches out from a radio nearby.

A knock at the door, then: "Pizza."

"Sanchez?" she says when I open the door. In her mid-twenties and in sweats, with a face that still could go either way: towards beauty and character, towards plainness, a kind of vacancy. Her nose is peeling from recent sunburn. Hair tucked into a long-billed baseball cap. "Comes to eleven ninety-seven."

I hand over a ten and a five and tell her to keep it.

"Have a good stay," she tells me in return. Her car is

an ancient VW beetle, once beige, in other incarnations green and canary yellow. There's a sign on top, FREE DE-LIVERY, that's almost as big as the car itself. In a good wind you could use it to sail the thing.

Under the pizza there are two waxed envelopes.

The first one contains a dossier on Luc Planchat. I know a lot of this, up till about ten years ago, and go through it hurriedly. There's a gap then for most of that ten years until, six months ago, entries resume.

Planchat had been the pride of a new program estab-lished in one of those backwashes we learn to live with, hawkish after several years of a kindler, gentler leader-ship. Someone with sufficient political clout had decided the only answer to terrorism was an elite killer corps and went about calling in sufficient favors to make it happen. Planchat was first car off the assembly line, the prototype, a real dazzler. He was also a loner. And became ever more so as his fellow grads started checking out to brute crazi-ness: some suddenly proclaiming themselves free agents (as though they were, after all, only football players), many either on their own or with a little help from their friends back at the factory heading out in search of what Rabelais called *le grand peut-être*.

The ensuing backwash was liberal, of course. When word came down that his program was deactivated, Plan-chat declined further government service and, in time-honored tradition, fostered out to a new identity.

Of three program graduates still undocumented (agency code meaning *not dead*), that accounted for two, Planchat and myself. Meanwhile "out in the world some-where" (as an old blues song has it), whereabouts un-known, identity unknown—if indeed he were still alive—there might be another. No one could be sure.

No one had an explanation, either, for Planchat's sudden resurfacing. All these years he'd quietly gone about his placebo life of employment, possessions, payments, polls, appointments. Then *something* brought him crashing back out of the closet.

Twenty-three weeks ago two security guards were found dead at Compso, a high-tech electronics manufacturer and research facility in upstate New York. Both had been dispatched instantly, expertly: the first with a single blow, the second by severing the spinal cord through a narrow incision at the base of his neck. There were some blinds and red herrings thrown up, but whatever was missing, *really* missing, didn't show up on any of the company's various inventories.

Four days later a military installation was hit; and in following weeks bodies turned up in hotel rooms, places of business, parks and storage facilities, warehouses, even once in a library. There was nothing definite to tie Planchat to any of this, but his name came up in one of those sotto voce conversations between our best jockey and his computer, and the more it was looked into, the more it started looking like a match.

For one thing, Planchat wasn't where he was supposed to be, and hadn't been there for a while—about six months.

He may as well have dropped off the edge of the earth, floated away in a balloon, gone to Tahiti to live among natives. Or been collected by extraterrestrials. The few spoors that existed were being tracked. Several calls had been traced to a phone booth in Dallas. That's why I'd been routed through here on my way in. To connect, if a connection existed. If the arc was there.

Rain hasn't abated. I put the dossier down and look again out the window. The world remains obscure. An occasional car scales the curved back of the hill like a momentary moon.

In that rented room of mine, the second month after I'd quit maybe, or the third, I got up one morning and, sitting still naked on the side of the bed, with frost plating the window outside and my own breath spilling out from me in spumes as a portable heater filled the room with the smell of raw alcohol, began a journal.

At first I simply transcribed my day: what I read and saw, where I went, stray thoughts, observations. Before long, though, I found the journal pulling away from the day's details and pastimes.

Memory was strong then; I sank back into it. Scenes of my childhood, friends, family, the way spaghetti or milk and oatmeal cookies had tasted when I was a kid, the first time I kissed a girl (Trudy Mayfield, Friday after school, February 1962), stories about a bibliographic worm in *Boy's Life,* my mother's face. It all came back in a flood.

Cedar Hill, I wrote. A two-story white frame house at the end of the block, with a scraggly weeping willow out front. We never locked doors, didn't even have keys for them as far as I know. Ate at a gray Formica table in the kitchen; the dining room stayed closed off except for holidays. A '52 Dodge with green plastic shades for the wing windows and windshield, and fluid drive. *Pecans.* They were everywhere, forever rolling and cracking open underfoot. Wasps in thick bushes that skirted the house. *Honeysuckle.*

But soon I learned that, precise and detailed as my memories were, they were also in some incomprehensible way complete. Once I had gone over a period in my mind, it was set; if I returned to it, there'd be nothing more, just those same memories. There was no depth.

There were also curious gaps. I could visualize my mother's face exactly, curve of cheek into chin, the winglike sweep of eyebrows, but I couldn't, for all my efforts, recall how she smelled, or the touch of her skin. And Trudy Mayfield's name was just that: a name. I had no image of her face, no further memories of her sitting beside me in a classroom or over sloppy joes in the school cafeteria.

Shortly after these realizations, I put the journal away. Best not to think about it, I told myself. I had a present, a life that gradually was taking on form, and *that* was what was important. Not the past, not history, not the stumbles and snags of a faulty memory.

I go into the bathroom, tear the weightless plastic cup out of its paper cocoon, fill it from the tap, and drink. When I come back, the couple (threesome?) next door has again taken up the challenge.

The second envelope contains a copy of the police report on the death of one Raymond Hicks, discovered by his common-law wife early that morning in their home on Colorado. The only mark on Mr. Hicks was a small incision beneath his nipple by way of which, with some flexible knifelike object and what the ME called "astonishing surgical skill," the ventricles of his heart had been pared away like quarters of an apple.

Rain streams on the window. Momentarily I feel like some ancient aquatic being, sequestered from evolution's progress in the depths of its cave and forgotten. When a truck's lights break suddenly against the rain there, I'm startled.

Raymond Hicks was the name Howard the Horse had given me back in Memphis.

8

IT'S GOOD TO SEE YOU.

"How long . . . ?"

Three years.

"What happened?"

Beats me. Woke up one day and turned over to say good morning to whoever was there and I couldn't. Now I write on this blackboard, like some kid. Nothing wrong physically, the doctors say. Hell, Dave, I'm sixty-two: there's a lot wrong physically.

"So at this advanced age you've become a writer."

Ha. It ain't funny, I guess. But then if it ain't funny, what the hell is it?

"Life."

Yeah, life. Joke without a punch line. So how you been?

"Good, Blaise. It was rough at first."

Letting go, you mean.

"Yes."

It was hard taking hold at first, too. You forget?

"No, I haven't forgotten. Anything. Including the fact that I wouldn't be here now, probably wouldn't have returned from my second assignment and certainly not from my tenth, if it hadn't been for you."

So you're welcome. You *have someone to tell good morning?*

"Yes. Her name's Gabrielle."

Good. That's important. You never did before. Maybe someday I'll get a chance to meet her. You can take us both to dinner.

"I'd like that."

You'd like it a lot more after a few years of the oatmeal soup here.

"I hope you're kidding."

With croutons. Just a guess, of course. Can't tell a thing by looking at it, even less from tasting it. You ever get around to reading that Frenchman I told you about?

"Cendrars—your namesake. Some of it. What I could find in translation. Amazing stuff."

Amazing life. What are you *doing these days?*

"I'm an artist, Blaise."

Always were. Saw it in you from the first. Told Johnsson that.

"A different kind of artist."

Different, huh? Everybody's hard behind change these days. Like there's always been something wrong with us and we just noticed it so now we're going to do something about it. People and things all changing so fast you can't hold on to any of them anymore.

"I never could."

Yeah. I guess maybe none of us could.

"Are you doing okay?"

I'm not doing at all—that's the problem. But yeah, I have what I need. Johnsson and the others, they see to that. He bring you in because of Luc?

"Yes, sir."

Thought he would. You still that *kind of artist too?*

"You mean, am I going to pull Luc down for him?"

It wouldn't be for him.

"Should I?"

You never asked me before what you should or shouldn't do.

"A dangerous word."

?

"Johnsson called *should* 'a most dangerous word.' "

He's right. But if you take out all the shoulds, what's left that's worth anything?

"I have to go, Blaise. Take care."

You too. Come again.

"I will. And next time I won't wait so long."

I may not wait at all. Ha.

9

I'M CERTAIN I am dreaming, and am watching, I think, within the dream, a play.

Scattered about the stage are folding screens, all of them sheer and lit from behind, some plain linen or rice paper, others painted with landscapes, domestic scenes, still lifes, vegetation. As actors speak and move about on-stage, they pass behind these screens, sometimes pausing there, other times moving quickly through, and reemerge. Whenever an actor goes behind a screen (beyond a country hillside, behind a table and chairs or a vase with flowers, among the silhouettes of a crowded street) the actor abruptly, unpredictably changes: how he moves, how he responds, what he says—veering off even in midphrase. A comic line suddenly gleams with menace, dialogue curdles to diatribe, an actor's kindly query concerning another's affairs becomes, for the split second he passes behind one of the screens, a fierce, mad monologue. When the actor reemerges then, just as suddenly, the play comes back to keel.

I look down and find I am holding a program. On its front is printed the play's title: *Dailyness*. On its back is a peel-off sticker reading HELLO MY NAME IS.

Applause starts up around me. An actor reemerges from one of the screens and the play, whose end he had signaled with a final, summary line while there, resumes.

10

"YES, DAVID."

I looked past the window at a group of young people emerging from Wendy's. They wore the general uniform of the day—jeans or baggy trousers, various combinations of T-shirts, denim jackets and oversize sweaters—and were laughing before the jokes got told.

"I just had an interesting conversation on the subject of change."

He had picked up the phone on the first ring. Now he waited a moment and said, "I see. Philosophical discussion, like memories, in time of inactivity can prove somewhat comforting, I suppose."

"Or, again like those memories, disturbing."

"Of course."

The young people, who'd gone out of frame to the right, reappeared in the window imaginatively arranged on the seats of a convertible. They were still laughing. On the wall by the phone someone had written in purple marker: WE NO WHO YOU R.

"I'll need a complete file," I said. "Not the one everybody else sees. Your own."

"Certainly, David. For whatever good it may do you. Which I suspect will be very little, by the way. But I'll have Lawrence run off a disk for you. Your preference as to format? ASCII, perhaps?"

"Paper."

"Very well. Paper, then. Those thrilling days of yesteryear. What else?"

"Clothes. All I have are jeans, sweatshirts, running shoes. Those won't do, not for this."

"Of course. Your measurements would be approximately as before, I assume."

"Close enough."

"Cohen is still with us. I believe he should be able to assemble what's required in short order. Suits for daytime and evening, I would think. Assorted sportswear. Formal?"

"Not for the moment."

"Very well. Shall I have Miss Sidney contact you about travel bookings, then?"

"I'll be driving."

"Driving. I see. Well: as you wish. Have you a preference as to automobile? Fiats are no longer readily available, you understand."

"Anything small and manageable, unflashy. With more power than it looks to have."

"I'll have such a car at your hotel within the hour. Keys will be at the front desk. You will find suitable clothing, an array of it, within the car. And should you need anything more, anything at all, simply call me. You'll be put through instantly."

"Thank you."

There was a low humming in the wires behind our

voices, like the voices of all those who came before us.

"I need to know if there's a timetable to this," I said.

"*Our* calendar's open. Intrinsically there may be. We don't know where all this is pointing, of course."

"If anywhere."

A brief pause? "Of course."

"One stipulation."

"Yes?"

"I don't want anyone flying up my butt on this one, sir."

"Department policy—"

"I know department policy, sir, the ones you broadcast and the ones your agents actually follow. I'm telling you that I go out alone, completely alone, or I don't go out at all. And that if I should happen to find someone behind me, I'll assume he doesn't belong there. Once I decide that, he won't *be* there."

"Understood."

"There's one more thing."

"Yes."

"I want a book sent. Poems by Cesare Pavese."

"To Gabrielle."

"Yes. I can't give you an address. I don't want to know, and I don't want anyone *else* to know. No direct contact or inquiry, nothing at all that might be traced. But the agency can find her and get the book to her discreetly. She'll know who sent it."

"Of course she will. David."

"Yes, sir."

"It's good to have you back. I know that Blaise was pleased to see you again after all this time. Thank you for going to see him."

"It accomplished what you wanted, at least."

"Nine years ago I would not have had to do that."
Someone spoke. He turned away momentarily to answer,
turned back. "But then, nine years ago it would not have
worked."

11

Assume there is purpose, connection, because you must start somewhere.

Assume the features we obtain connecting these dots, these aleatory islands, are those of Luc Planchat, though in fact they may not be.

Assume that a line drawn through the coordinates of my motel-room visit in Memphis and the death of Raymond Hicks in Dallas necessarily intersects other events past and future, bearing them all towards pattern, *completion, closure.*

Things of the world try to connect. Prodigal rain issues from a sky into which trees rise like pleading hands. Days bear us lightly across the face of the world as every year the ground pulls harder, recalling like a spurned lover, ever more fixedly, how much it wants us.

Across that same grid (as on the screens of my dream) fall the contours of my own history and future, here congruent, there fugitive, the configuration of *my* face a Venn diagram overlaying *his,* Planchat's.

He knows. The Memphis motel-room visit and Hicks's death signaled that. And while I have little knowledge of the past ten years, of what Luc has become, how he thinks and what might be important to him, I know intimately the rise and fall of far deeper sensibilities.

Essentially (*au fond,* as Blaise might have said) we're the same.

I have only to wait.

12

ONCE IN FRANCE I waited three days in a blind alley among decaying trash, battling rats and ravaged, ravenous birds for a certain man to walk past, as sooner or later he *had* to walk by, that alley's mouth. I lived on stale bread and a foot-long sausage I'd carried in with me. It rained fitfully, and I collected what water I could for drinking. On the fourth day, near sunset, all my preparations began to gather into a single, sudden thrust—then instinctively, for reasons I still don't know, stopped—as the man for whom I'd waited stepped into sight. I crossed the border back into Germany that same night. And months later, far from there and assigned to matters wholly unrelated, discovered that our information had been, in one small detail, wrong. Had I pulled my target down that day, it would have proved a terrible mistake.

13

I n many ways, of course, the clothing available to me determined my role, and though it filled only two small-ish leather bags, I should now be able, with middling imagination and care, to graze at whatever social level I required. Cohen was something of a genius in that regard, author of one slim, esoteric book, *Dress: Code and Language,* that brought him to the agency's attention. I often wonder if his fellow academics ever noticed he was gone and thought to question what might have happened to him.

The car was an excellent choice as well, a midseventies 240Z in workabout condition that might just as easily be (considering my age) a leftover from college days or a vintage piece in the throes of restoration. There were patches of primer and the whole thing was an odd bluish-gray that looked as much like undercoat as paint; wheels were mismatched; the passenger door hung askew.

Saying good-bye once again to Baltimore, I threw both suitcases and my own cloth book bag in the back of the Datsun and started out of town along the Loop in no particular direction with no destination in mind.

Away from Baltimore, Washington and this whole stretch of tucked-in coast. And most of all just *moving*. Two things about moving targets. First, they're harder to hit. Second, they get noticed a hell of a lot quicker.

I stopped at a service plaza, bought maps of the northwest states and Florida and paid with a fifty-dollar bill, even putting the faintest, indefinable trace of an East-European accent in my voice to be sure I'd be remembered. Reflexes come back fast. Red herrings, feints. The mutability of it all.

I was wearing jeans, leather deck shoes and a cotton sweater without a shirt, sleeves pushed up to my elbows. I'd purposefully not shaved that morning. There was a sedate black watch on my wrist, a calfskin trifold wallet in my left rear pocket.

I had curved slowly inland from coastal routes, and highways here coursed through unbroken stands of trees—oak and maple, birch, elm—with little indication of the towns and communities one knew lay beyond. Only a monotonous cadence of exit signs with icons for GAS, FOOD, DIESEL, RESTROOMS, and every few miles the mast of a gas-station sign rising out of the trees. As though the six-lane interstate had materialized here to allow visitors from other places, possibly from other worlds or times, to experience what this country once was like everywhere: its rawness and awesome scale; how empty it had been, and at the same time how filled. Yet these thickets of growth were Potemkin blinds. Depart the interstate, and you found they shortly gave way to sprawling settlements of Texacos, Exxons, Kwik Stops, Mc-Donalds.

The hills themselves seemed every bit as redundant as

the exits, swelling up gradually, monotonously, under prow, then settling in a languid curve towards the next.

An hour or so outside D.C., I topped one of those hills into the most astonishing sunset I've ever seen. Somehow I'd taken a turn out of real life into a movie, a travel brochure, a romantic novel. I pulled to the side of the road and sat with the motor off, watching. When the last fire-struck tendrils darkened to slate and let go, I felt a sense of personal longing and loss, a bristling sadness.

Deep into Virginia, wonder of wonders, I found an FM station that followed some classic Louis Armstrong/Bessie Smith with a Ravel piano concerto and an a cappella quartet version of Neil Young's "After the Gold Rush."

Once, a deer staggered into the wash of my headlights, turned and sprang away.

Other eyes glittered from the growth at road's edge.

Bodies of raccoons, dogs, opossum, a lone porcupine, lay at roadside.

Around ten I stopped to eat. A special section of the café (with a phone in each booth) was reserved expressly for truckers whose rigs circled the gravel-and-asphalt parking lot like wagons in old Westerns. Rack upon rack of bright postcards, novelty items, NoDoz, eyeglass cleaner, lighters and pocket knives bearing the Confederate flag. Tattooed arms and huge bellies in black T-shirts crowded around a rack of Books on Tape: Louis L'Amour, Stephen King, technothrillers. Little doubt I was in the heartland of America.

An LED banner-box set over the rear counter scrolled by news headlines, aphorisms and self-improvement for the benefit of the truckers as they ate. The Word for the Day was *eschatology*.

My barley-and-beef soup was good, the cornbread even better. Afterwards I had a piece of pecan pie and dawdled over two cups of coffee trying to decide whether to drive on or crash for the night at the motel *(Rooms Scientifically Cooled)* across the street.

"Passing through, honey?" the waitress said when she brought more coffee. I'm fairly sure I had never in my life been called honey before this. She was thirtyish, virtually blond, with features you'd forget once you looked away. A woman who had made a sudden stop on the way to pretty, who would never quite get over how close she'd been. A white plastic rectangle over one high breast read *Alicia*.

I nodded.

"Well, should you have a taste for a cocktail or two, there's this little place just down the road, Lou's, you can't beat." She gestured across at the motel. "And you won't do better than the Island anywhere within ninety miles of here if you need a place to sleep. If you're of a mind, that is. My husband—ex-husband I should say, really—runs it like a cruise ship. I should know, I put in my share of sixteen- and eighteen-hour days over there. Anything else I can get you?"

I told her no, and thanks.

"You change your mind, we're open all night. I'll be here to twelve, myself."

Alicia waited a moment, put down the check and walked away.

Lou's was everything I could have hoped for, though

I almost missed it on my first pass since the neon sign overhead read BLUE CORRAL. But a wooden one in the window said *Lou's,* and that was also painted above the front door in the same DayGlo green.

Basically it was a feeding trough: bar running down the middle of a long shotgun room, with slots for livestock, or in this case stools, on either side. Pool tables floated in their islands of light off in the darkness to one side, a dance floor lined with stacked plastic chairs loomed to the other.

I took a stool near the door beside a cowboy who looked like something from a wax museum and asked for a beer. Out in darkness on the dance-floor side, a guitarist and bass player tuned by harmonics. A dancing couple, the man forty or more and wearing slacks with white shirt and tie, his partner maybe half his age and wearing considerably less than half a T-shirt and jeans, periodically orbited into the bar's dim light and back out into blackness.

I drank my beer and asked for another. The cowboy was drinking coffee with bourbon in it. He had a little squeeze bottle of honey in his pocket and was putting some of that into the cup too.

After a while, having made the round of drinkers, the bartender came back over and stood across from me. He was as quietly animated and as flushed with color as the cowboy was waxlike.

"Lou," he said, sticking his hand across the bar.

I took it. "Dave."

"Good to have you. Haven't seen you in here before, I don't think."

"Haven't had the chance."

He nodded. "Quiet night. There's usually a good group in here, though, most nights. Come in here either to drink and be left alone, or else to dance. Either way, mostly they don't get to minding somebody else's business."

I told him I knew what he meant.

"Not like some places. You want a shot with that beer, maybe? Be on the house, you understand, first-time customer and all."

"Thanks, but I'll stick with beer. I'm not much of a drinker. Just unwinding a little. You know."

"On the road."

I nodded, and he nodded back. Two good old boys who knew what a man had to go through.

There was a loud thump from out of the darkness, then a voice:

"All right, you rebels, cowboys, horsewomen, Jaycees, JDs and all others within the sound of my voice." A pause, an adjustment. "Keep those cards and letters comin' in. And if you have a request, so do we: keep it to yourself."

Lights came up slowly onstage. A portly, youngish man stood there with a high-slung hollowbody electric. He wore preppy clothes—sweater, broadcloth shirt, tan chinos—and a cowboy hat. Behind him in shadow, as though they belonged to one another, shadow and musician, the bass player half-sat on a bar stool, ragged out in honestly worn jeans with a sateen tour jacket, hair to his shoulders, a single long earring.

There was a sudden, machine-gun-like burst of hot jazz guitar.

"Okay, Justin, we're ready if you are. All saddled up up here. Let's *ride,* man."

The cowboy on the stool beside me looked at me for the first time.

"Boy's your basic asshole," he said, "but if there's a better guitar player in four states I ain't seen him."

He got up, ambled onstage, strapped on a bright red electric mandolin.

"Keep it country," he said, "just keep it country," and the band broke into an uptempo version of "Faded Love" heavy on tremolo and sevenths. They worked without a drummer, and with that particular bass player, with the guitarist somehow laying in brick-solid rhythm chords and skirting all around the melody at the same time, they didn't have much need for one.

"Faded Love" gave way to "Sweet Georgia Brown" and that to a breakneck "Jolie Blonde." Then a catchall of current hits with the guitarist singing while the mandolin player stitched bluesy licks and fills all through his lyrics.

Sometime during the second set and third beer, the bar stool beside me stopped being empty.

"Okay if I join you?" Alicia said. "Guess you changed your mind huh? God, I love these guys. Bourbon and water, Lou."

She had changed into black jeans, pink hightop canvas shoes, a voluminous man's cardigan (sleeves rolled into doughnuts) over a lowcut cotton top. What appeared to be an authentic Indian arrowhead hung from a rawhide thong and pointed down into her cleavage.

Foucault's pendulum. Use it to deduce and demonstrate the earth's rotation.

"We haven't really met," she said, "but I'm Alicia. You're staying at the Island, too, I bet. Business trip, or pleasure?"

"Business, mostly."

"You ever mix the two?"

I shrugged, and the gesture hung between us there in the air like a ghost struggling to keep its form, like a diminutive fire. She smiled and took a healthy swig of her drink, then a measured one. Accustomed to pacing out a night's drinking.

"Well," she said. "You like country music?"

I nodded.

"You don't look like you would. Not the type, you know? And so much of it's just junk anyhow. I'm gonna get drunk till I get over you. Kick me again, that's the only time we touch. But then in the middle of it all there'll be this one line, or this few seconds of music, that's just absolutely right, that says what *you* need to say in ways you never can."

We had a couple more drinks and sat there talking. Alicia was twenty-eight, legally married but living on her own for about two years now, in furnished apartments mostly, sometimes with a dog, God she loved dogs, but the dogs, like the men, never lasted. They all ran away or turned mean.

We agreed on one last drink, and towards the end of it she said: "Guess you must be pretty tired huh, being on the road and all. Prob'ly just going to go on back to your room and turn in."

I told her that I was.

"Yeah. Well, me too, I guess."

We said good-bye and I walked out into the parking

lot, leaving the start of a new set and "Milkcow Blues" behind. An older man in a bowling shirt leaned against the wall puking. A jet whistled past overhead. The neon BLUE CORRAL sign flickered once and became BLUE COR AL. Lost at sea.

Not long after, there was a knock at my motel-room door. I opened it. She was carrying her sweater.

"This is absolutely your last chance," Alicia said. She looked beyond me into the room and smiled: "Or mine."

14

OUTSIDE A TOWN named Stonebrook I pulled off the interstate, stopped at a U-Halt convenience store and at the pay phone there dialed a number that shuttled me through several blind relays and redirects before ringing.

The phone was picked up without greeting.

"Sir," I said, "perhaps you remember Marek Obtułowicz. Also used the name Lev Aaronson. We worked together in Gdansk, then again for a stretch in Santiago."

"Yes. Went to ground some years back. In Budapest, if I remember. We were never able to confirm."

"I've been thinking about something he often said, an old Russian proverb: Do not call in a wolf when dogs attack you."

He waited a moment. "I see. This is the reason you have called on a secure field line, against every policy and all standard practice."

"Yes."

"Then let me offer in return something my father read to me when I was a child. It is from Karl Kraus, I believe. 'To be sure, the dog is loyal. But why, on that account, should we take him as an example? He is loyal to men, not to other dogs.' Is there anything else?"

"No, sir."

"Stay in touch, David."

And the connection was gone.

I stood watching a bluebottle fly throw itself again and again at the window, buzzing furiously. The sill was lined with the desiccating husks of its predecessors.

15

THE ROAD GIVES us release, reaffirms the discontinuity of our lives, whispers to us that we are after all free, that (around this curve, when we reach the next town, if we can only make it to California) things will change. Twain and Kerouac both knew the great American novel would have to be a book of the road. So did James Fenimore Cooper, before there *were* roads.

When I left the agency, I sank almost my whole severance pay into a car. Since the agency took care of our needs, I'd never been in a position to accumulate things—clothing, automobile, house, apartment—and that car became virtually all I had. It was perforce, for several months, where I lived: a late-fifties Buick with auxiliary gas tank and custom sound, backseat scooped out to make room for sleeping and cargo. And in it I drove from Memphis to Dallas to Akron to Seattle, often reaching my destination only to turn around and start back or veer off towards yet another fanciful destination, spending nights at the side of wayward country roads or in motels that sprang up sudden and solitary as cactus along Oklahoma highways. And always in those months, music was playing: big bands, Bessie Smith, Bix, Trane, Eric Dolphy. Being on the road, and music, were all that made sense to me for a while.

And so I drove southward now, and westward, thinking of Alicia across from me at the diner that morning. I had the radio tuned to a comedy hour. Jokes about wives, dogs, kids, bosses, kumquats, kangaroos. All equally alien to me. An absolutely impenetrable five minutes of double-talk on contemporary relationships from "The Professor of Desire."

"You ever be back through here?" Alicia had said, watching me over her coffee cup.

I shook my head.

"Yeah. Well, I didn't think you would be. No way. But that's all right."

The waitress brought our breakfasts and asked Alicia if she worked today. Off, she answered, but I have to pull the night-owl tomorrow.

"There's something in you," Alicia said when she was gone, "something you keep hidden. Dangerous, maybe. And maybe that's why I wanted to know you. But it wouldn't matter how well or how long I knew you, would it? That something would always stay hidden."

"There's something hidden in all of us."

"Dangerous things?"

"For many of us, anyway. Even if we don't recognize them, or know they're there."

We finished our breakfast and coffee and said goodbye outside by the car. There's never a lot you can say at times like that, apartness spreading like a stain between you, sky dumping its endless spaces over your head.

Alicia had touched my arm, very softly, and gone back into the diner.

My reveries were interrupted (again!) by rude reality, this time in the form of a battered gray Chevy. It dropped onto me outside a town called Carl's Bay, dogged me past the town's dozen or so roadside buildings, and finally announced intentions as we passed a city-limits sign and started into a long curve that quickly bore the town out of sight.

The Chevy came up fast on the inside. I saw only the driver. It wasn't Planchat, of course, or anyone I knew; it wouldn't be. But obviously there wasn't enough road for both of us. Out of town by sundown and all that.

The obligatory car chase was taking place rather early on in the movie.

There are several ways you can handle this sort of thing. Probably the best is just to ignore it, and that's what I did for some time, the Chevy's driver growing ever more reckless and erratic, like a bull throwing itself repeatedly at the same stretch of steel fence.

He came up alongside and made as though to swerve into me. Dropped back till I could barely see him, then all at once closed the distance and shot around. Pulled off to the roadside and waited, rocking the car on its rear wheels, as I went by.

Another response is to bail out, just refuse to play, and when I thought the time was right, the stew just about ready for serving, *that's* what I did.

I braked, neither fast nor slow, and came to a stop in the road.

The Chevy's driver zipped on by, braked hard with an eye on the rearview mirror, then tried a fancy turn and almost lost it. The Chevy sat facing me about thirty yards down the road.

I waved.

Then I floored the little Datsun, feeling everything it had cut in, and headed straight for him.

I was outweighed by at least a ton and would have wound up crushed against his grill like a bug, but reflex won out. I watched him haul the Chevy hard right and, in the rearview, saw him try to bring it back around and fail. It went over on its side, then heavily onto its back in the roadside ditch.

Saw it start to, saw it had to, saw it happen, as Archibald MacLeish wrote.

Everything was very still.

This is where the audience whoops it up for the good guy, I told myself.

But there weren't any cheers or applause. Only more road waiting to unwind, most of a day left to unwind it, and god knows what waiting ahead.

I slowed again and drove on.

It was the sixties, a woman said on the radio, and I decided to drop out, *really* drop out. I went down to Sears and bought me a sleeping bag, a camp stove, some heavy boots. Gave everything else away to friends. Then I hitched out to the middle of Montana with everything I owned stuffed into a backpack. Found this neat cave. Moved in. Lived there four days in absolute, wonderful solitude; and on the fifth day the bear came back.

16

I ONCE READ a story by this guy named Harlan Ellison ending: That night it rained, everywhere in the known universe. I was never too sure what the ending meant in terms of Ellison's story, but anyone who sits alone in a motel room for hours, watching rain wash the world away, begins to understand. Knows what it *feels* like.

I'd lost the Chevy and later in the day, with appreciably more finesse and less violence, another car, a recent Buick; but I had little doubt the stalking continued. He was (they were) out there somewhere in all that water, in what remained of the world, what hadn't been washed away, waiting.

A coded call from another phone booth, though not on a secure field line this time, had brought information at best equivocal: no further incidents involving Planchat, no further sign of him. Presumably I was the distraction from whatever program he'd previously been pursuing. And presumably it was Planchat, or his soldiers, dogging me: *I* was the program now. Just as I wanted.

I'd driven into Helena (pop. 11,972, all nice people, it said so right there on the sign) in a downpour. There were two motels, one at either end of town, the Sleep Inn and The Deluxe, and I chose the latter, then went back out to sea for provisions.

After me, the deluge? Well, it sure *seemed* to be after me.

I sat on the swayback bed eating canned ham, water crackers and longhorn cheese and watching reruns of old TV shows about humble crises within happy families. Each was resolved when a character decided to do what he or she had known all along to be the right thing. There weren't a lot of families left, happy or otherwise, among the people I knew. And very few people seemed to know what was the right thing to do.

I shifted the dial over to FM music and drew a bath so hot my skin reddened. I soaked in it till the water grew cold, through sets of Buddy Holly, the Beatles and the Talking Heads, then came out and lay on the bed. It was seven-thirty. Lots of night left to fill. No letup in the rain.

Back a few months before I met Gabrielle, for a short while, there had been someone else, a young woman named Carol whom I met in a used bookstore. She was in line ahead of me with a stack of science fiction and bi-ographies and needed forty-two cents. We had coffee at the lunch counter of a drugstore nearby. I followed her home.

Carol lived about as close to the ground as anyone I'd known, in the beachlike expanse of an unreconstructed second-floor commercial loft relieved only by five or six folding chairs, upended crates, an exercise mat she used as a bed, a scatter of bright cotton rugs. Walls were hung with photographs of the city's many baffles and dead ends, and of its denizens. Often there would be a dozen or more versions of the same subject, a battered face, an alleyway opening onto dark sky, each so like the others that only with close examination could I discern subtle shifts in angle or focus, in lighting, in contrast.

Carol had put on water for more coffee and a Tom Waits album. Listening to "Tom Traubert's Blues" there beside her in what was more akin to the waiting room of a train station than a place where someone actually lived, so aware of her, so taken by a woman's softness and scent after so long, buzzed with the coffee we'd already drunk, I was overcome by Waits's music, by the way he became what he sang. By the all but unendurable pain in his voice and the petty, doomed heroism of his people.

We listened to a lot of Waits that summer. It was a world I knew all too well, a world of bars and bleak mornings, of forfeits and endless beginnings-over that never took. A world Carol was courting.

To create his music, to give that world voice, Waits had transformed himself as unmercifully as did castrati or Rimbaud, burrowing ever deeper into the city dweller's brutish, subterranean, neon-struck life. And so, for similar reason, did Carol. I never knew whether art or access to that world was her primary motivation: if the photographs were intended somehow to earn her entry, or if perhaps she had come to believe her assumption into that world essential to continuing, to perfecting, her art. At any rate, she followed in Waits's wake, turning away from privilege, family, comfort and safety to live in poverty and to spend her nights roaming the city's black heart, her days slogging down hard coffee and (as she said again and again of her work) *trying to get it right.*

I don't know if she ever got it right. But that world,

or some other, did finally open and let her fully in: one morning she didn't come back to the loft, and I never saw her again. In a way, I think, I'd been expecting it. But for a long time I went on looking down into the street half-thinking she would be there; for a long time I listened for the sound of her feet on steel stairs. I waited, there in the loft that later became my own studio. And now, far away from there, I remember.

17

DAWN WAS ROSY-FINGERED, just like in Homer. But did someone want it bloody?

Waking every hour or so from old habit, I had been aware of the rain's slow passing. By five, when I came fully awake, it was over. By six I was on the road.

I drove for a couple of hours before stopping for toast and tea at a café, Sam's, in the middle, possibly on the edge, of nowhere. Nowhere consisted of Sam's, a gas station and a dance hall. The gas station and the dance hall weren't open.

Oddly enough, Sam's was almost filled.

Or maybe that wasn't so odd, considering the choices available.

I sat over my tea—a generic bag of English Breakfast loosely packed with leaves as dry and brittle as insect legs, all they had—and listened to splinters of conversation, trying to reconstruct in my mind something of the lives around me.

I was, I supposed, in the very heartland of America now, among people whose values, families and bottom-line way of life I had been protecting in all my years, in all my actions, with the agency. A quarrelsome dictator removed here, a cooperative military junta supplied with weapons there, an assassination or two. Eyes-only information passed along, overthrows, "tactical support." All so that (nominally, at least) these people could go on about their lives of Budweiser, proms, sitcoms, Saturday-night football and Sunday church. They'd never know about most of it, of course, and if they did, would never understand. One of the reasons—just one—that I felt so terribly apart from them.

I was still in that contemplative frame of mind thirty or forty miles down the road when the holes appeared in my windshield.

There was no sound or real sense of impact, only two sudden holes about the diameter of pencils, spaced an inch or so apart, slightly to my right. I looked down at foam protruding from the seat just above my shoulder where one of the loads had entered. It looked like a small flower.

I pulled off into a patch of sunlight and killed the engine, not so much looking or listening for anything in particular as simply *opening* myself: becoming a receptacle for whatever sensation might fall in.

Why had I had no indications at all, no premonition?

A raucous flight of birds overhead. An approaching semi. The purr of other engines far off.

Nothing that shouldn't be here, as far as I could see or sense.

No Hollywood glint of steel in the trees or hills.

Ten minutes passed.

I was reaching down to turn the key when two more holes appeared in the windshield, this time to my left, again an inch or so apart.

Two flowers in the seat beside me.

Basically, if someone wants to kill you, if he's any good at it at all—if, say, he's an expert marksman, as this guy seems to be—and especially with current technology, there's not a lot you can do about it.

I got out and stood by the car, breathing deeply, feeling muscles let go. It's a trick you learn, at first. Then it becomes a reflexive response.

Nothing . . .

Sunlight and silence.

Against the horizon a frail-looking biplane skimmed the top of remnant clouds.

Of course, if he *doesn't* want to kill you, you may have to wonder why he's making such a show of trying to.

I got back in the Datsun and started the engine. Switched the radio on and sat there. "Sympathy for the Devil": *bamboula* drums, shouts. Called *hocketing* back in Senegambia.

A hawk dived from a nearby treetop and swept low over the Datsun, banking.

No new holes or flowers.

18

I stopped at the next town and made a great pretense of looking for an old college friend. Asked after him at a diner and gas station, made several phone calls, kept going back to the car to rummage through the glove compartment and my book bag. Even cruised streets for a while at 20 mph, slowing still further to rubberneck infrequent signs at corners.

As illusionist Howard Thurston used to tell his assistants: If you don't know what's going on, boy, just smile and point the other way.

Soldiers and dinosaurs like myself wouldn't be so easily misdirected, of course, but I wasn't certain just who I was dealing with, not yet, and this could be one way of finding out. Besides, confusion never goes to waste. And it gets to be almost instinctive after a while. All part of the game, chords to play choruses over, steps of the ritual dance we locked ourselves into again and again.

"C'mon, m'am," I said at the local post office. "Give a guy some help here, all right? We go *way* back. Jimmie—with an *i-e*, not a *y*. Never James: Jim. Last name sounded English. You know? I mean, I can see his face like it was yesterday. Parkingham? Markham?"

"The postal service is not a public information system, sir." Visions of long, untroubled breaks, lunches replete with fried-shrimp po-boys, and a fine, secure retirement filled her head.

"I know that, m'am. And I know you guys do one hell of a job. Women too, of course. But hey, this is the first chance I've had to look him up in almost twenty years. It ain't like I'm calling in from home to ask you something. I'm standing right here, and I just drove over four hundred miles, and tomorrow I gotta drive at least that again. Just don't tell me I'm gonna have to go all the way back to Portland without ever seeing my old buddy after all this, okay? Just don't tell me that."

I stared off (fiercely? forlornly?) towards the window. Some double-winged insect the size of a hummingbird butted away at it.

"Hey, hold on a minute. *Berkeley*. That's it! We all used to call him Bish. *Esse es percipi,* the eraser, what eraser? and all that. How could I have forgotten?"

"I'm happy for you, sir. Have a safe and pleasant journey home."

"C'mon, m'am. Miss? Jimmie Berkeley. How hard is it? I'm begging you. Bail me out here, huh? Whatta we have, if we don't have our memories?"

And wouldn't you know, with all the other towns I might have pulled into, with the name itself (or so I thought) pure invention, just riding way out there on the edge of a blue note, there actually would *be* a Jimmie Berkeley in Marvell, North Carolina.

"I really should call my supervisor—"

"Please. Please do. Absolutely. In your place I'd do the same."

"—but I can't see the harm in it."

"Maybe you should call him anyway? For appearance's sake. Cover your bases."

"And things haven't been going at all well for Jimmie this past few years. It should do him good to see an old friend, talk over better times."

Johnsson's *should*. That dangerous word again.

"He's living out at the old Swensen place. Caretaking. Not that there's any care to take, or much left to take care of. What do you call it? A sinecure?"

She sketched lightly on the back of an old envelope as she went on.

"The mailing address is route one, box nine. But the way you get there is to take Cherry, that's the main street out front,"—as a bold line crossed the bottom of her improvised page—"on up to Loman's Lane and turn right once you pass the Nazarene church." A square with a cross inside it. "Then you go on four, five miles. Till you come to an old boarded-up Spur station. That'll be on your right. The road to the left's the one you want, the gravel one." Thinner lines now. "Half a mile more, over the creek, first house you come to. First one you'll *see,* anyhow. Out behind the big house, where old Swensen lived, there's a cottage, probably used to be a carriage house or slave's quarters. That's Jimmie's place." An *X.*

Remaining in character, I thanked her effusively, all the time thinking *Damn, damn, damn,* and *What webs we weave.*

But like a good athlete, now I had to follow through.

I had to go out there, shoot the basket, fumble, trip, foul and withdraw.

So I did.

Jimmie climbed down off a tractor overgrown with vines at the edge of trees as I came up the drive. The ruts coming in were bad enough, but these were worse. I lumbered over them, the low-slung Datsun bottoming out again and again, hood heaving up and crashing back down like a ship in heavy sea. I hit the brake and rocked to a stop. Jimmie stood by the big house waiting.

Okay. I'd indulge in a few moments' small talk and tell him sorry, obviously I have the wrong person. Wrong town, maybe. Completion, closure. Then back the Z up, U-turn, and get the hell out of there.

But I saw in his eyes, or thought I saw, some trace of recognition. And something about his face, something in the pace and cadence of his words, was familiar.

"Can I help you, sir?" he said, keeping a distance.

"I . . . I seem to have lost my way. Can you tell me how to get back to the interstate?"

"Well, I reckon you're lost all right. Leastways the *highway* is." He laughed. "But you just turn around and go on back down the way you came a few miles, and when you fetch up against the creek, you turn left. Don't you cross the creek, now, just turn *at* it. Mile or two farther along, you'll see your highway."

"Got it. Thanks."

He stepped closer to the car.

"I know you?"

"Don't see how."

"Not from these parts, then?"

"No."

"And I been here my whole life. But I do know you. We've met up before." He shook his head and shrugged. "In some other life, maybe. Who knows about these things? You okay now on finding your highway?"

I said yes, thanked him again and sailed back down the ruts.

Who indeed knows?

As I'd told the postal clerk, before this man I thought I was making up out of whole cloth took on flesh and spoke to me: What do we have if we don't have our memories?

What I believed pure invention had become *more,* seemed in fact to have made its way to the surface from some clandestine well of memory.

What if memory itself, in turn—his, my own—were only invention?

19

For the next hundred miles a Ford Escort moved up to number one on the charts.

Talk about protective coloration. A Ford *Escort?*

It picked me up not long after Carl's Bay and the unseen sniper. A Dodge van had come around some miles back, so for a while it was a toss-up, both with a bullet, as they say, but then the van turned off and never came back, meaning either that it didn't figure at all, or that it was running a classic A-B tail and had passed me on to the Ford.

So that's the song we were dancing to.

I drove along thinking of those first weeks in the Buick following my retirement, the endless miles of highway I covered and recovered, all the open road I had felt beginning to unfurl in my mind and life, Brubeck and Bird and Sidney Bechet unwinding on the tape player the whole time. That stuff wasn't readily available then; I'd paid dearly to have collectors dub it for me from their stashes of old records and acetates.

I thought of men long since dead, of a woman's face in Chile, of part of a child I found beside the road one morning in Salvador. I remembered what it felt like when someone died there beside you, how your own body became in that instant instantly more real, more alive.

I wondered what use a soldier with a conscience could possibly be, and if indeed I had one (but I was here, wasn't I?), and what conscience was.

No more trustworthy, no less unreconstructed, perhaps, than was memory?

Just after lunch the Escort ceded favor to a Mazda pickup that paced me at such a calm distance I became certain I was this time in the presence of a pro.

Mazda sat uncomplaining in a vacant lot the whole while I stretched a steakhouse dinner to almost two hours. When I left, it came along quietly. And when I went to ground, it pulled into the parking lot between tourist cabin number nine and the sole exit.

Fair enough.

He knew the moves without having to work them out. I was no longer dealing with amateurs.

The cabins were pure fifties postcard: fake frontier, as though some Titan's idiot child had been given a set of Lincoln Logs for Christmas and turned loose, complete with brown plastic chimneys and slab doors painted to look like four planks with crossties. Inside, it was even worse. You could barely turn around in there without bumping into *something;* it was packed full with a green Naugahyde sofa and chair, a bed whose headboard put one in mind of tombstones, matching blond dresser and bureau, a corner desk shelled with aqua Formica that after many years of bondage and struggle had almost succeeded in emancipating itself from its support brackets.

I used the cabin's phone and my own calling card to send a telegram to a deadfall address: *Xanadu tomorrow stop.*

More confusion and background noise.

I left open the canvas curtain with its frontier scenes—wagon wheels, lariats, a chuck wagon—and turned on the TV to a Special Report about recent mass murders in Utah. Canted newsreel footage of the suspect, of abandoned backyards and one-time schoolrooms, of a town square, a storm-laden sky. Interviews with a psychologist specializing in (caps? italics?) the criminal mind and with, unaccountably, a "television consultant." (A *what?*) Having become instantly, momentarily, an actor, each spoke his lines with heavy sadness and certitude. Apparently it occurred to no one that, inasmuch as explanations and answers *did* exist, they were complex ones, and might only be found in the suspensions of true discourse or of art, certainly not in homilies, slogans, threadbare aphorisms.

Strike another blow, I thought inanely, for American no-how.

The newscast was followed by a poorly dubbed Japanese mystery, *Ransom,* that nevertheless immediately swept me up and carried me off, more from the intensity of the lead character's features and the stark, angular black and white of the film itself—like something out of his own mind—than for any facility of plot or technique.

A three-time murderer (though none of them committed in passion), Osho is released from prison during war with the understanding that, in return for his freedom, he will kill again: this time a most peculiar patriot, an old, once-great soldier now leading his people away from confrontation and towards negotiation. Osho instead flees, settling in an obscure mountain village where he becomes protector for a young, mildly retarded woman with whom he falls slowly in love, and for her family. Raiders—refugees from various war zones, deserted soldiers—periodically come upon the village by chance only to be dispatched, violently, by Osho. There are brief flashbacks to beatings he received from his father as a child; to (at the beginning of this same war) the imposition of martial law and subsequent confiscation of his home village's sole source of income, its fishing boats; to the single boat he and a friend carried into the hills and the officer they struck and happened to kill when he came upon them there; to the man whose throat he slit years later in a barroom brawl over a woman whose name he never knew or asked; to the face of a man he almost killed, but from whom he drew back at the last moment, in prison. By film's end, despite all he has done, despite his final, passionate killing, one feels a great compassion, a spilling tenderness, for Osho. In the movie's last frames, half a dozen policemen in plainclothes climb slowly up the mountain to put him to death for defaulting on his bargain. The country is at peace.

I walked to the window, half-expecting the Mazda's driver to be in the window opposite looking back, the same film coming to its end on the screen behind him.

But there was only blackness out there, blackness shot through from time to time with the lash of passing lights, broken by the dull thunder of trucks on the interstate a mile away.

And behind, there was only more news, more detective shows and sitcoms, endless advertising, an interminable hour of sophomoric British comedy in tuxedos and drag.

I slept well, dreaming of the countryside of southern France, its small *caves* and restaurants, its pâtés, oversize bottles of local wine, cassoulets, greens and rolling green hills. I was a leaf carried along by wind. Wind whispered softly to me and would never grow tired. *Ma feuille,* the wind said, *ma petite feuille, ma jolie feuille . . .*

In the morning, no less surprised than I might have been upon receiving, by return post, a reply to a message in a bottle, or to words whispered into the darkness, I received a response to my telegram.

"Mr. Anderson?" the desk clerk said when I picked up the phone. He was probably also owner, maintenance man and half the housekeeping staff. "I'm sorry about disturbing you at such an early hour, but I have a telegram here for you."

"Yes?"

"You want me to read it?"

"Please."

"Oh. Okay. Let's see . . . it says: *I await you.* And there's something else here, a name maybe. *K-U-B-L-A?* That's it. Be checking out this morning, will you?"

"Yes. Thanks again."

"Oh no: thank *you.*"

Ten minutes later, the Mazda pulled out behind me. We drove up the street like a very small circus and stopped at a truck stop for breakfast. Plenty of parking in front. This time he came in, sat at the counter and ordered coffee.

20

I ATE BREAKFAST slowly and, afterwards, carried a second cup of coffee over to the counter and sat beside him. He was on his third or fourth, with milk and with sweetener from sky-blue packages. Where we were, you could see stacks of glasses in wire racks against the kitchen wall, a tottering tray of napkins rolled, burrito-like, around silverware, a badly encrusted waffle iron.

"Come here often?"

A lot younger than I would have thought—but aren't they all?—and good-looking in some indefinably continental way; functionally dressed in loose jeans, sweater, ski jacket, running shoes. I wasn't the only one who thought him good-looking. The waitress spent an inordinate amount of time seeing to his coffee.

"Capricorn," he said. "And no, I don't want to dance."

We sat there a while. Truckers came in, made calls over coffee and burgers and left. Travelers whose children could be seen looming into the windows of vans outside like sharks in aquariums materialized at the counter and voyaged back out with cartons of food in hand.

"So what do we do next?" I said. "You supposed to smother me with a jelly doughnut?"

"Thought maybe I'd just persuade you to order the chili. That ought to do it."

"Or I could jot down my itinerary, we'd meet a couple of times a day for meals. Save you a lot of trouble. Easier for everybody, in the long run."

"Hmmmm," he said, and got more coffee from the waitress. Can't let a good customer take two sips without a refill. He nodded to her and smiled.

"We could even consider carpooling," I said. "I can't remember if there's an energy crisis right now, but if not, one's bound to be along shortly."

He shook his head, half an inch in either direction, once. "Don't think so. I've seen the way you drive."

"There's that. But you do have to look at the big picture."

He looked into his coffee instead and suggested a walk. I paid, waited as he spoke with the waitress, then we went out together into a chill, sunny morning. Sunlight on everything, just lying there, trying to get warm.

We walked down the main stretch a block or two, then onto a side street that barely managed to harbor six buildings and a building-size, overgrown parking lot before surrendering to the chaos of kudzu and what people hereabouts called *woods*. I'd had similar feelings once on a brief assignment in Midland-Odessa, Texas: this sense that three paces out from the city I'd step abruptly off the continental shelf, into quicksand and nothingness—as though aliens had carved the city from its environs and deposited it here.

"Do you remember a morning in the fall of '71, on Cyprus?" my companion said after a time.

A woman's face floated into my mind. The smell of lemon trees, kerosene.

"I do. But there's no way *you* could."

He went on. "Because of your presence, because of what you did, or caused to happen, there—I don't know the details of this, and you yourself may or may not recall them—a woman selected to die instead was reunited with her children."

Oh, yes: I remembered.

"Years later, far from those islands, in a far different life, in a different world, that woman again found love and remarried. Her husband was a Russian émigré, a childless widower who had long believed his life over, his family name never to be forwarded, his fortunes at an end.

"Dmitri was at first astonished, then grateful, to find love and family so late in his course. Gratitude did not come easy to him, you understand. He had clawed his way up from the rudest dock work. It was difficult for him to credit fortune, chance, destiny—to credit *anything* but his own determination and labor—for what happened in his life. And because that recognition, that gratitude, came with such difficulty, it was taken most seriously. Taken *to his heart,* as he himself might say. It became one of the central facts of his life.

"In time that gratitude extended itself to the person he knew to be responsible for his wife's survival. And so, declaring someday that person would be properly thanked, Dmitri turned his considerable resources towards discovering the man's identity."

My companion paused, watching an Amish buggy make its plodding way along the road's shoulder.

"It was, as I'm sure you know, a for*mid*able task."

Stressed on the second syllable, as the British do.

"I'd think so." Hope so.

"One fraught with false trails, laden with dead ends, blinds, misdirections. And impossible to say, finally, whether it was dogged persistence, money—vast sums of it, pirate chests full of it—or simple luck that's carried me at last to this long-desired end."

"This is the end, then? Here?"

"The Russian, Dmitri, died many years ago—as good a man as will ever see this world. His wife, the woman you knew as Cybelle, followed shortly after.

"In thanking you now, I discharge both my father's gratitude and the vow I made to him.

"*Spaseba,*" he said, holding out his hand. "I am Michael. And now, I suppose, finally, I can get on with my life."

Thinking of his obvious professionalism, I said:

"But surely this *is* your life."

"No. I'm an engineer, a shipbuilder, actually. Not that I've had much chance to practice that profession."

We had come back around to the truck stop.

"For all his efforts and dedication, the old Russian was never able to discover your identity. In fact he learned almost nothing. What else was there for me, then, but to become, myself, what we knew you to be? If you wish to find wolves, *become* a wolf.

"This is what I did. I trained and had myself sent out

as a field agent and before long in that clandestine, circumspect world I began encountering certain . . . stories, I suppose you would say. You may or may not know: a kind of myth, a hollowness, exists in the place you once occupied. As in Voznesensky's poem for Robert Lowell:

встал в пустоту, что осталась от роста Петра.

"You were ensconced, shrouded, in that space. But then it began to seem as though the space might be no longer vacant, the hollowness filling. Rumbles of far-off thunder made their way to me. Rumors, unexplained occurrences, movements on the horizon. All of which led me inexorably to this assignment. To you. And thereby to the end of one career."

We stood near a huge plate-glass door plastered over with travel stickers. Our breath pedaled out into the chill morning air. A middle-aged couple on a Gold Wing pulled up at the curb and sat with engine idling, studying separate maps, he in half-moon reading glasses, she holding the map out away from her, squinting.

"I had assumed it was *my* career that was supposed to end," I said. "And my life."

"So, apparently, had others." Michael looked into the café. The waitress looked back at him from behind the counter. They both smiled.

"I must tell you: I am not at all certain that I recognize the game pieces in use here, or that I know their proper moves. And the board itself seems a most peculiar, oddly shaped one. I hope that you will take particular caution, my friend."

He held out his hand and we shook.

"How very strange to call you that: friend. You have been central to my life for much of it. Yet I've not met you until this day. And now will have no reason to see you again."

"Unless you come simply *as* a friend."

I stood for a moment watching through a tiny map of Texas on the door as he reentered the café and sat at the counter. A cup of coffee was put before him. The waitress, apparently, was on break; she came and sat beside him.

21

For the remainder of that day and much of the next—presumably until someone got around to discovering Michael's apostasy—I was a solo act. Sailing free and alone on the interstate and through adjunct towns, at peace with myself and surroundings.

Then about three in the afternoon, roughly alongside a stretch of fiberglass hot tubs turned on edge like huge jigsaw pieces and another service-road store selling "chainsaw art" (totemlike figures of bears and other wildlife liberated waist- or haunch-up from tree trunks), with acquisition of a sporty little white job and a mooselike Pontiac—countertenor, bass—I became a trio.

They took the Datsun out an hour or so later.

There wasn't a lot I could do. We'd cat-and-moused for thirty miles or more on the straightaway before nosing into a cluster of tight, contradictory curves. The Pontiac had lugged up hard on my outside then, holding me in the curves and crowding close against me while the sports car, a Fiat, nipped and nibbled at the inside like a good cow dog.

It was all timed perfectly, almost balletic. And when

finally I did leave the road—more or less electively, as it happened, taking what I decided might well be my last chance—for a moment, just before the rear wheels lost purchase, I thought I'd done it, thought I might actually have pulled it off.

The Datsun hit the far bank and paused, listing for an interminable moment during which several Latin American nations changed their names, political ideology and rulers at least once, then, very rapidly, gaining speed all the while, began rolling.

After six it all seemed academic and I quit counting.

So I started rolling, myself: out of the tight ball I'd tucked myself into and out of the car in a single ongoing motion. Then let momentum carry me onto my feet and sprinted between billboards for steak houses, motels and wrecker services into nearby trees.

I was on a limb high overhead when they finally talked themselves into coming in after me. I could see their cars pulled into a gap-toothed V back at roadside. There were only the two drivers, one a middle-aged, crewcut man in crisp white shirt, tie and windbreaker, the other in Yuppie Lumberjack and baseball cap. The older one had a shotgun. The younger one probably thought his red shirt was weapon enough.

I stayed up there a long while, letting them wear themselves down and lose what edge they had.

Then the kid stepped around a tree into my elbow and went down. His head lay propped against roots. Blood poured from his nose and pooled at his collar, soaking into the shirt, darkening it to maroon. He snored.

The older one was considerably more trouble, and for a time I was afraid I'd moved on him too hard. But eventually light seeped back into the dull gray eyes he leveled at me.

I nodded to him.

After a moment he said: "Correct me if I'm wrong. But I suppose if I move—if I can, that is—you'll shoot me."

"With what?"

I was sitting, knees up, against a tree. I spread my hands.

"Okay if I sit up? Again: if I can."

I nodded.

He came up slowly, hands flat against legs, breathing deeply, forcing the pain back. Put it in the pantry, use it later.

"Adrian?" he said.

"Asleep."

"Temporarily, or otherwise?"

"Give him half an hour."

He looked off towards the highway, blinked up at the sun through the canopy of leaves. A squirrel was fussing up there somewhere.

"Right, then."

He lifted his left hand and probed at its wrist, experimentally, dispassionately, with the fingers of the other.

"Third time now I've broken the sucker. So . . ."

He looked at me again. Eyes depthless.

"So?" I said.

"So what's the deal?"

"How about we play History? I'm the big bad Russians and you're Julius Rosenberg. Tell me some secrets."

"Yeah, well, I know how that one ended."

"This one doesn't have to."

There was a sudden exodus of birds from trees around us. Moments later, half a block long, a truck heaved into view on the service road, cab black and gleaming, bright cars lashed to scaffolding behind, distinct as paints in a paintbox.

"Cigarettes in my shirt," he said. "All right if I get them?"

"Sure."

He lit one and sat smoking, watching the truck swing back onto the interstate. I thought of camels lumbering among dunes half a world away. Of Erector Sets, carnival rides, the Eiffel Tower. My sculpture.

"Can't help you much. There's this man—an agent, I guess you'd have to call him. No pun intended. Everything comes through him. Someone needs a job done, he gets in touch, and the man sets terms, strikes the bargain. I call in later, a couple of times a day when I'm not already working, otherwise it might be two or three before I get a chance, and he tells me go here or there. Be in Dallas at five, Akron tomorrow morning, this is what you have to do there. Tickets are always waiting for me. Motel rooms. Cash. Everything about it ultraclean, professional. Smooth. So I can't give you a name. That's why it's all set up the way it is."

He shook his head. "The rest is silence," he said.

But it wasn't.

Adrian's breathing signaled trouble. We both heard the laboring heaves, listened and caught the gasp, realized at the same moment that his breathing had stopped.

And suddenly were there, together, at the tree.

Grabbing ankles, I pulled the boy down flat and

thumped at his chest, twice, hard, with a fist. Then quickly measured three fingers up from the xiphoid, locked fingers and began rocking, elbows stiff.

"One thousand, two thousand . . ."

His companion pinched nostrils shut and blew his own breath into Adrian's mouth.

"Three thousand, four thousand, five . . ."

Breath.

"One thousand, two . . ."

Breath.

"One thousand . . ."

Breath.

Nothing.

After ten or twelve minutes, on *change,* we traded places. I watched him there above the boy rock back and forth on his one good hand, counting; and every fifth compression I blew my own breath forcibly into Adrian's still mouth. It remained still. Our sweat fell onto him.

We shifted places, shifted again.

Until finally, exhausted, we gave up. Adrian's pupils had been dilated for some time.

"What the hell happened?" my co-rescuer said.

"No way to know," I said. "I'm sorry."

"Yeah. Well." He lit a cigarette and fell back against the roots, breathing hard, looking up at sky. "It's all pretty frail, what holds us here."

"You got kids?" he said after a while.

I shook my head.

"Wife?"

No.

"Not many of us do. Boy there's the closest I was ever

gonna come. Twenty-one years old. Would of been twenty-two next month. You even remember what it was like, being that young?"

Not really.

"Me either."

He struggled to his feet and to the Pontiac, fished a bottle of Stoly out of the glove compartment and brought it back.

"Join me?" he said.

We passed the bottle back and forth a few times.

"I don't get out much," he said. "You know how it is, working all the time, never knowing where you might wake up tomorrow morning. Then I *do* get out, and I look at all these people with their suits and their station wagons and the next thirty years of their life stamped out like it's on the back of a coin, and I have to wonder what makes them go on.

"Has to be family, I figure. And I guess Adrian there was pretty much *my* last chance for family."

I handed the bottle across.

He took a small, careful sip and passed it back to me.

I finished it off. Held the bottle close to me. Birds sang again. We sat there a while without talking.

"Come on," he said. "Help me get the boy into the car and I'll give you a lift to the next town. Get on with our lives, as they say."

As if we had them: lives.

22

Not that, before this, it hadn't been "real" to me.

It was real: I'd seen too many bodies, too many cities gnawed at by flame, too many blank faces and shut-down lives, for it to be anything less. But until that moment my own two lives—the old one, which had embraced these things, which was defined by them; and the new, which at first denied them, later and at best strove somehow to understand them, to incorporate them, to absorb them—had not come together.

Like an eye exam where letters right and left loom wrenchingly out of focus, then suddenly swim towards one another and lock together.

Irony, some would say, is the voice of our time, a time perhaps more given to image, to form, than to substance. And it's difficult to imagine any more ironic image than two veteran killers squatting there at roadside trying to resuscitate a younger, unseasoned version of themselves.

A fever in my bones, Pavese might have said.

It began, truly began, there.

Images swam in my mind. But they swam beneath a dark membrane. I could make out only the faintest outlines of their forms as momentarily they tugged upward, tugged against that surface, then rebounded into the depths.

Premonitions? Memories? Occult understandings?

Trying to escape, to break out—whatever they were. As do we all.

Given paper and crayon, the ape draws, laboriously, precisely, only the bars of its cage, again and again.

23

ADRIAN'S MENTOR DROPPED me at a phone booth on the edge of the next town. Johnsson answered on the second ring:

"Again, David, I must ask that you stop calling on secure lines."

"You had no way of knowing who this would be."

"Chances were quite good. One develops a feel for that sort of thing, you may recall."

"I need a priority-one check."

"Actually, David, that's the only kind we do in these days of computerized files. But go ahead."

I told him about my conversation in the café, no more than I had to.

"Michael. The last name may be Danyovich. Father, Dmitri. Mother was Cyprus-born, name unknown, though at one time in her life she used Cybelle."

I described Michael as only a trained observer can (albeit a long-unpracticed one) and told Johnsson that I'd stand by. I started to give him the number but he said he had no need of it: that the technology was a bit further along these days. I opened the phone booth door for air and watched traffic ease itself along the two-lane street. Within ten minutes, Johnsson rang back.

"Of several names," he began without preamble, "I find that of Michael Kandinsky—sometimes Michel, or Mikhail—most often used. He matches your description and, as far as we can trace things, the background you sketched. A fairly new player, it would seem. And an extremely cautious one. Almost no tabs to pull."

"Affiliation?"

"Freelance, like most of the East Europeans these days. They— Hold on."

Absolute silence on the line, with every twenty seconds the high-pitched bleep of the sweeper.

"David, the computer's latched onto something else. It's scrolling up now. . . .

"Apparently some years ago, still in his teens, your young man found himself in trouble while on holiday in Turkey. Smoked a couple of joints with his girlfriend and a few of the wrong people, it seems. Spent a most unfortunate week in prison there before his father located and, handing over generous sums of *baksheesh,* retrieved him. The girlfriend was never heard from again. Inquiries were made through channels, officials denied any knowledge, the usual folderol."

"Not all that unusual a story, as I recall."

"No. But a year or so later, three guards at that same prison were found flayed and hung upside down on poles just outside the gates. Caused a bit of a stir, even for those times."

"Could it be coincidence?"

"It *could* be, as you well know, anything. A familial grudge, a military power struggle, depletion of the ozone layer. I myself am no strong believer in coincidence, however."

"He's insane."

"Perhaps. Remarkably motivated, certainly. The young man returned from that Turkish prison and, with his father's virtually unlimited funds, went back to school with a vengeance—though his major had changed.

"Over the following years we can track a stream of mercenaries, martial-arts teachers, munitions and surveillance experts, athletic trainers, gentlemen in our own line of work both active and retired, even a terrorist or two, to and from various locations about the world. We would never have been able to discern a pattern, before this; the activities appeared random. With Michael as fulcrum, however, tracing everything back to him, the pattern emerges."

"He turned himself into one of us."

"So it would seem."

"But why? Surely not all that, simply for revenge?"

"Actually, the incident with the guards seems to have been more or less incidental. Something of an advanced training mission, perhaps: who knows?"

I knew, of course—if what Michael had told me was in fact true.

"After that incident," Johnsson went on, "we keep losing the spoor. Michael becomes in effect virtually invisible, surfacing here or there at will and—again—apparently at random, then quickly resubmerging. There are glimpses of him in Santiago, some intimation of a lengthy assignment in Rio, a possible walk-on in Puerto Rico."

"Where does Planchat fit into all this? Assuming that he does."

"Only two roles are possible, David."

"Hunter or hunted, you mean."

"Quite."

"There might be another."

He waited. I heard, twice, the bleep of the sweeper.

"Mentor," I said. "He might have been one of Michael's teachers."

Three, four, five bleeps went by.

"Yes," Johnsson said. "Unlikely. But possible."

Three more.

"There has been no further indication of Planchat's presence. Were we the sort of men who make assumptions, we might assume him to be out of the picture."

"You think Michael brought him down, then?"

"Of course we are *not* that sort."

"Or that it's all been Michael, all along?"

That it was Michael I'd been hunting from the first—or allowing to hunt me—made no sense. But then, not much else did, either.

"That is a possibility," Johnsson said. "One there had been no reason to consider before this."

"So what do we do?"

"There may be little left that we *can* do just now. Your instinct, obviously, is that Michael should not be brought down?"

"At this time: yes. What I *feel* is that Michael's truly out of the picture now. But if not, then he's so deeply imbedded that, once we gouge him out of it, there's no picture left."

"In which case . . ."

"I will continue as before."

"Yes. That is almost certainly best."

Two bleeps. Three.

"So very much activity," Johnsson said, "and to so little apparent purpose. Every light in town is on. And still we are able to see so little."

Or in his case (I remembered suddenly) nothing.

"One thing further, David."

"Yes?"

"Your friend. Gabrielle. It seems that everything is getting gathered up in this tangle. Perhaps you'd best attend to her safety?"

24

I walked up the street to Norma's Cafe and went in, remembering the beginning of *The Postman Always Rings Twice*. At Norma's, food seemed to be pretty much an afterthought. Instead of dishes there were mostly beer cans. The *spécialité de la maison* was Bud Light.

I asked for coffee and got something reasonably close. On the counter nearby, a glass bell preserved half a cake passed down, from Norma to Norma, by untold generations of the cafe's owners. Lift the bell away and the cake would crumble to dust.

I sat sipping at my coffee. Two elderly men played checkers at a rickety back table. Neither one made a move the whole time I sat there. But every minute or two, again and again, from one side of the board or the other a hand would reach out, pause over pieces, and withdraw.

After a while, most of the Cherokee nation came over and sat beside me.

He was at least six-six, easily three-fifty without the boots and belt buckle that would add another twenty pounds or so. He wore a baseball cap, baggy fatigues with a lot of feathers hanging off. I was pretty sure the stool had groaned when he settled onto it.

He sat smiling at me. Two sips of coffee went by, never to be seen again.

"You remember how it was, man? You do. I can tell. How they'd hunker down out there by the fires for hours while bugs crawled all over your rice and boiled grass and in the corner you always tried to get to before you had to shit. Nothing on their faces, man. Absolutely nothing. That's what I remember. Faces smooth and blank as stones in a riverbed. And they'd rock a little on their heels out there by the fires. Looking like birds. Even sounded like them. And finally you'd just give up and eat the slop, bugs and all."

He shrugged. Planes flying overhead may have encountered turbulence.

"Fuck that shit. That's what I say. Just fuck it. Am I right?"

I told him he was.

"Fuckin' *A*," he said, and drank a few more beers while I had a sip of coffee.

"We're Asians too, man—you know that? Fuckin' *walked* here's what we did. Everything was still connected back then. And we could of walked anywhere, you know? But *this* is where we wound up, this was our country. Then you U-rope-peons heard about the buffalo and came over here thinkin' you could have yourself cheap steaks for dinner ever'day and fucked it all up. Just like you fucked up Nam."

Everything in the cafe got very quiet. I could hear the flame popping beneath the grill.

"You ain't listening, man. And I thought you knew

what I was *saying* to you here. Thought maybe you might even care a little. It could happen. But fuckitall: you're just like the rest."

He had another beer to prepare himself for what had to be done. Then he turned to do it—but I wasn't there. So he kept on turning, to where I stood behind him. Still on the stool, he threw an off-balance right that, inches away as I moved, slammed air against my eardrum and left it ringing.

I rolled in a slow circle around the punch, coming back in just as it peaked, adding my own momentum to his. He went along, then somersaulted away from me, unfolded, and slid four or five feet across the floor flat on his back. He would have slid further, but the café's tables were bolted down, and the second one stopped him.

"All *right!*" he said, and there was a general exodus towards the far wall as he got up.

It lasted longer than it should have. Finally I did manage to drop him without getting hurt myself or, more important, without having to kill or seriously maim my opponent, but it wasn't easy. And it took a while.

After the second tumble, he climbed back to his feet and left brute force, all he'd ever needed for civilian life, there on the floor.

He'd been well and thoroughly trained, and had grafted that training onto what was probably from the first a strong natural aptitude. As I watched now, trying to get a handle on what he was likely to do, he was either weightless and gliding, or he was solid stone. Nothing in between. And the edge came back to him then. I could see the difference behind his eyes, in the way he began moving. As though sharks had swum into the goldfish tank.

I'd go in for feints, just enough to get him moving, then roll away, out of reach.

Like a lot of fighters trained by the armed forces, he was strictly a full-out man: all offense and attack, every movement revved up till the metal screamed, every blow delivered like a bomb.

So I dogged it, made him keep coming after me. Got in close enough for him to strike and rolled off it when he did, looking to be much more affected than I was. I even stumbled once or twice. And then when he came in the last time, low, to shut me down, I wheeled around him and went back off the wall with both legs, adding my own weight and momentum to his, and rode him headfirst into the stainless-steel lunch counter.

The waiter set another coffee down in front of me.

"That happen very often?" I asked him.

"Never more'n a couple times a day. 'Cept Saturdays, of course. Indian's flat crazy."

"Nam was a bitch."

"Probably so. But Lee there was flat crazy 'fore he went."

"Is there anyone we should call to see after him? A wife, maybe?"

"Lee done killed one wife and run at least two others off. But I expect someone'll be along shortly."

He nodded at my cup.

"Better hurry and finish your coffee," he said.

25

Heavy in the hindquarters, with his small, sharp face, J. B. Pickett reminded me of a rodent standing erect. He was stooped, head bent down and forward, and his hands moved all the time. His skin was the color of flour sacks, hair brown and lifeless. He was, he told me, "the law" around here. He was also the Indian's half-brother.

"You can flat fight, that's for sure. Ain't nobody stomped Lee in a good long time." He poured coffee for both of us, into ceramic mugs, and handed one to me. His said *Roy*. Mine said *Dale*. "Reckon the last one who did was me."

We sat at what served for his desk, an old pine table with gouges and grooves polished smooth as marble and saturated with half a century's oils and cleaners. School libraries used to have these tables. Now they have particle board. Hot air poured in through an open, screenless window. So did endless streams of unhappy insects.

The law blew across his cup, blinked at the steam when it rolled back in. Every inch polite, professional and proper, but I couldn't shake the feeling that on a slow day he might sign up for lessons at the Arthur Murray Studios for the chance to step on toes.

"Just passing through, I guess."

I nodded.

"Headin' anywhere in particular?"

The first three words ran together in a long slur. The last one's syllables were ticked off in cadence, *par-tic-u-lar,* like a banker counting out bills.

"Not really. New Orleans, eventually."

I hadn't known that until I said it, but realized it was true.

"*Coming* from anywhere in particular, then?"

"Last stop was Boston."

"Boston. I was up that way once."

He tugged a Styrofoam cooler from under the desk, nudged the top aside and took out a pint carton of Half 'n' Half. Held it towards me and, when I shook my head, dumped some in his coffee.

"You have a car, Mr. Edwards?"

He replaced carton in cooler, cooler beneath desk.

"I've been hitching several days now. I'd hoped I might find new transportation around here, though. Something inexpensive and more or less dependable. If anything like that exists."

"I 'spect you'd be likely to find something, if you were to look. You have a job, Mr. Edwards?"

"Self-employed."

"You prove that?"

"Do I need to?"

"Might." He leaned forward, chair springs groaning.

"Let me tell you what came to me. You want some more coffee?"

I held the cup up to indicate that plenty remained.

"Came to me that, first, you don't look much like your standard hitcher, if you know what I mean. And that you knew just a little too much about what you were doing in there up against Lee. Came to me that you might be a person someone was looking for, and if so, that I ought to know about that. You able to follow my thinking?"

I nodded. I was following it all too well.

He leaned back in the chair again, springs sighing with relief.

"I was able to lift the better part of three good prints off that cup of coffee you had over to Norma's. Friend of mine who works up in the capital, I had him run those prints for me. Have any notion what he might have turned up?"

I drank some coffee. Waited.

"Well, his computer kicked the prints and ID right out, no problem: *David Edwards*. Along with a dossier it pulled in from various linkages on the data system. But my friend wasn't satisfied with what he got. Said it was too easy, too quick and clean, that he got more than he asked for. That made him suspicious. And the more he thought about it, the more it bothered him. So *he* called in a favor—these guys all know one another, I gather— and piggybacked on a system that's tied into some pretty obscure, and exclusive, data banks. Privileged, my friend put it. Shielded."

Without asking, he got up and poured more coffee into my cup. Then refilled his own and put the glass carafe on the desk alongside. His chair wheezed like a laryngitic accordion as he settled back into it.

"A strange thing happened, Mr. Edwards. Whatever data banks my friend accessed—credit, military, census—he got back the same thing. *Exactly* the same thing. Said it reminded him of obituaries waiting in newspaper files. Three or four tight paragraphs set as though in cement, scattered facts giving no notion of a real life behind those names, places, dates. And he'd never had anything like that happen before. Never."

He held out the carafe to me and, when I declined, emptied the rest into his own cup.

"My friend has an awesome curiosity. Not for the information itself, you understand—actually he cares little at all for that—but for the getting of it. Says it's the only thing he's ever been good at. And so he dug in, blind as a mole, buried like a dung beetle, burrowing the contemporary world's *real* subterrain."

He drank coffee for a while, smiling across at me.

"Eventually, my friend tells me, he managed to find a few cracks, get his foot in a door or two. But then, almost as though his presence somehow had been detected, those doors slammed shut, all at the same instant. And he was left with only a glimpse, the barest intimations of something, a dissolving shape."

He looked into his cup, moved it in slow circles.

"How old are you, Mr. Edwards? What: late thirties? Forty?"

I picked an age at random. "Thirty-nine."

"Yet, up until nine years ago, your life's a fortune cookie."

I inclined my head slightly, asking that he go on,

inviting further information, by my own silence.

"I don't suppose there's a number I should call, anything like that?"

I shook my head.

"So," he said. "The horns of the moment's dilemma."

He looked towards the window. A wasp flew in, circled the room quickly and fled back outside.

"Obviously you'll provide me no information. Yet on the other hand I am enjoined, by my profession and by my charge to this community, to insist upon the answers I cannot have."

He leaned closer to me, arms flat on the table.

"Mr. Edwards. Are you willing, or able, at least to tell me what you're doing here?"

"I haven't misrepresented myself in any way, Sheriff, nor do I have reason to do so. I truly am just passing through. There's no more to it than that."

"And if I should release you now, you would continue that passage?"

I nodded.

"Your presence here has nothing to do with Lee Raincrow?"

"Nothing."

He looked into my face. A kind of information beyond words, small tides of recognition, passed between us.

"Buy you a drink," he said shortly, rising. "Said you had need of a car, I believe?"

I nodded.

He nodded back. "Reckon I might know where you could locate one."

26

It was in a town called Cross, standing before an acrylic painting of a melting, chromatic city, that I became someone else.

It had happened before—once already this time out, in fact, with my to-be assassin in Memphis. I'd find myself in peril, nerve-ends singing, and suddenly everything out there would *change,* the world would shimmer, go away for a moment, come back transformed. But it had never before happened when I wasn't in clear, direct danger. And never before with such intensity.

I'd been reading signs for fifty miles or more, GREATER SOUTHEAST ART SHOW, rocking along in my VW bug the color of a perpetual bruise (someone had painted a dark-blue car maroon, badly), so when I finally got to Cross, subject of the signs, host to GSAS, I thought *why not?* and pulled into the parking lot of a Rodeway Inn festooned with plastic red, blue and gold banners.

Everyone in Cross was already there. Most of them seemed to be milling about the parking lot drinking beer. The rest were clustered around tables hurriedly pulled together in the coffee shop. A high school class and I pretty much had free run of the ballroom, where the artwork was on display.

It was largely what I might have expected: landscapes, a few still lifes, primitive portraits and rustic collage, some art-school pieces. Lots of flowers, trees and animals. Still, overall quality of technique was high. The edge wears just a little finer each year, it seems. And the quantity of work was truly astonishing. Had *everyone* turned into an artist of some sort?

The car, incidentally, was Lee Raincrow's. Lee had lost his license a while back, permanently this time, and (I was assured) would have no further need of the VW. I gave Pickett six hundred for it and figured if I got a mile per dollar out of it I'd still be ahead.

I had made a quick round of the ballroom and come back for a moment to the acrylic, getting set to leave, when it happened.

I have no idea how long it lasted. But I know it had been going on for some time when my own consciousness started filtering back in: dull clouds shot with light, bright threads, bright segments.

The painting was no longer there before me. I stood looking down through a rainswept window at the street. Someone stood behind me, almost touching.

"You're apart from me tonight," she said, and I turned to look at her. Hair cut short, boyish. Crimson lipstick and a T-shirt that fell to midthigh. "In some other kingdom?"

"I don't mean to be," I said as she moved into the embrace that waited for and fit her precisely. The heat of her skin sliding against my own.

The connection did not end there, not for a while.

Slowly I surfaced, at once a part of their coupling and divorced from it, observer, intruder, and when at last it was over, their bodies falling wordlessly beside one another on the bed *there,* the painting before me once again *here,* I must have felt much the same sense of loss and quiet sadness as they. It bore up like a wave beneath me, bringing thoughts of Gabrielle, of my recent and more distant past, of the solitude enclosing us all.

Fragmentary impressions, scraps of others' memories and others' thoughts, still clung to me: what had washed up on my shores.

27

So I drove out of the Rodeway Inn parking lot, out of Cross, with a biography forming, like images swimming up in a developing tray, ghostly at first, gradually, almost imperceptibly more substantial.

That biography, those memories, thus far were *only* images, images unaccompanied by words or understanding, images without referent. It was like being in a country whose language you know not at all. Or like being inside someone else's dream.

"I" was from farmland. A skittering impression of jade-green hills and deep-blue sky, the smell of damp hay, manure, compost, pollen, decay. Nights rimmed about with the sound of locust and crickets.

Then the sudden descent of cities, still photography giving way to cinema, everything speeding up, wheeling by, shooting away. A procession of women, university years, fine meals and wine in out-of-the-way, *recherché* cafes, hollow-eyed men peering out from dark doorways and from beneath bridges.

And beneath it all, a terrible undertow of despair, an

emptiness whose rim "I" often approached though "I" never looked fully in.

There was, with each woman, each bright moment, a strong sense of place as well. Hotel rooms mostly, the occasional *pension,* park or public square. Once a monastery of cloistered stone corridors damp with condensation.

So: "I" traveled often, "I" liked women and music and plain, freshly prepared foods. "I" preferred coffee so black and thick that Balzac would have passed it up. "I" swam whenever possible in icy waters. "I" was a man of discipline and exacting, though personal, principle.

And "I" circled like a hawk *my* erratic flight south, this fool's voyage, this floundering, freewheeling march from sea to dark sea.

28

It BROKE EVERY RULE, of course. But that, in a way, is what the agency's all about.

In flight training, for combat situations where you find yourself momentarily confused and unable to make split-second decisions, it's drilled into you over and over just to *do something,* anything, to start a sequence of events. And that pretty much defines us. We're the agency that *does something.*

I remember one time in the sixties some government body or another informed Johnsson that henceforth he would, *could,* send none of us into Central or South America without that body's express consent. Johnsson immediately posted every man in the agency to Panama. We all passed a pleasant three-week vacation there, filling Panama City's hotels, while back home they went about trying to untangle threads, blame, careers, feet, tongues.

The phone was ringing as I tossed luggage and book bag onto the bed in cabin six of The Cambridge Arms in Piltdown, Alabama. I picked it up, listened a moment and went back out, past the motel's corner office and down the street to a pay phone.

"Yes?"

"This is the rabbit returning Alice's call."

Neither of us spoke as computers swept the line.

"I'm afraid Alice has just stepped out."

I waited five minutes and called back. Anyone breaking into the line now would be shunted over to a recorded conversation.

"In the Bible in your room, second drawer of the bedside table, when you return," Johnsson said without preamble, "there will be a . . . document, that against all regulation and simple good sense I've caused to be forwarded on to you—only, I would add, because of the circumstances under which it arrived here, circumstances indicating that the document has a certain urgency, both to its sender and, I assume, to its recipient."

"Yes, sir."

"I will tell you also that the document appears to be truly blind. That we have been unable to trace its origin and route and thereby assume that no one else would be able to do so."

I waited. There was more, or he would have hung up. I listened to crackles in the wires, tiny electronic fires flaring up, draining away.

"Often those close to us know far more about us than we think, David. More than we wish them to know. That is, I suppose, in its own quiet way a danger. But it can also be a comfort."

This time he broke the connection. I caught a snatch of recorded conversation before that line, too, was released. Something about mountains and the timberline.

In the drawer alongside a long-out-of-date telephone directory and yellowing hotel stationery inexplicably bearing the crest of the old Fontainebleu in New Orleans, I found the Bible. Gideon checked out and left it no doubt. And in the divide between New and Old Testaments, a blue, unmarked envelope.

The letter began, as Johnsson had, without preamble.

All the things I might ordinarily say, I leave to the silence between us; but there are things even that silence will not bear.

You are altogether an extraordinary man, Dave. Gentle and strong, principled, supple—in many ways the most complete person I've ever known. And I do know that you have given yourself to me as never before with anyone else. But there has always been something else as well, a closed-up room inside you, an attic where long ago you put things away, whatever those things were, and never went back.

Often at night I would lie beside you, especially when we were first together, feeling the pain that you did not, would not, allow yourself to feel. With time that faded, as everything does; but it has become as much a part of me now as it is of you.

It doesn't matter how I discovered what little I actually know of your past. It was not knowledge I sought; but knowledge that came to me unbidden. Perhaps if we see one another again, if from that uncertain, unreal place we call the future, you return to me (and I must hold close to me the very real chance that you will not), this will become important, but it isn't now.

What *is* important is that you understand how I feel about you, about my life and your place in it. We never talked about such things much, or needed to. Maybe now we do. *I* do.

It's a warm, strangely undark night and I'm sitting outside on an old wood porch with wind in my hair (I cut it a few days ago), remembering your face that first day at the museum. Sometimes I think the only use the past has is to break our hearts. That memory makes me so happy, David— and so sad at the same time. Your face, and the sky so blue past the windows, and Matisse's circling dancers. The way everything *fit,* then.

It's becoming difficult to maintain belief that the world will ever right itself again, that somewhere there's a road leading back to that very small place, that clearing, we shared for a while.

I've been reading Pavese, yes. There's so much feeling in these poems, such a terrible, unforgiving sadness—and so much life. Real people walking everywhere inside them, carrying from place to place the ones they love.

I think that Pavese loved women as you love us. I see that his images of death—always wed to sensuous detail, the smell of rich earth, caress of wind bringing rain, curve of a woman's hip against the sky—are like your own, in your work. And I have to wonder exactly what your message may have been in sending this book.

I will be here, David, if you choose to return, and can. I won't be waiting, I'm not able to go on doing that, but I will be here.

There was no signature. Something within me, something that *was* me, had gone suddenly heavy, become a black sun pulling everything into it: matter, energy, even light.

Dearest Gabrielle, I wonder too what my message may have been.

I wonder how one ever learns to sort through and make sense of the messages, signs, signals, meanings coming down all the time on our heads, weighing on us, piling up about us. While we go on trying to guide these frail crafts, our lives, into harbors we never see yet fiercely believe, have to believe, are there.

Low in the water and listing from the burden of memories, I sat in The Cambridge Arms, Piltdown, Alabama, looking out on a small Confederate cemetery and, beyond, a bright ribbon of interstate.

29

PILTDOWN, AN EXACT replica of Oxford, England, had been created in the late forties by a man named Neal Lafferty who conjured it up out of whole cloth, creatio ex nihilo, a monument to man's indomitable will to be, well, indomitable.

Brought to you by the same people who at enormous, repetitive effort and expense filled in swampland never meant for human habitation and called it New Orleans.

Lafferty had stepped off the boat from Ireland poor as potatoes a couple generations before and within six years gone from helping build houses at a dollar a day to buying them up cheaply with his savings when the region's economy plummeted and, much later, reselling dear. When an air force base came to Piltdown, Lafferty's construction company got the housing contract and doubled the town's size with an eastward warren of dozens of identical little frame houses, row after row of them, like carrots in a garden.

The base lasted twelve years before peacetime shut it down, leaving the little houses a ghost town. Many of them were vandalized, others (host for migrant workers, vagabonds, late-night teenage parties) burned; they all were crumbling. Eventually Negroes moved in and claimed the houses by squatter's rights, plugging holes with tar paper, scrap lumber and old tin signs.

Lafferty then turned his attentions westward, where he built, to scale, a perfect replica of central Oxford, this by municipal decree some years later *becoming* Piltdown, leaving the old town hall, shops, post office and churches abandoned there at the edge of things like a shed skin, like so many cast-off shells.

No one knew why Lafferty had undertaken this massive and costly project, or why he might have chosen as model, of all places, Oxford; and he went to his deathbed without saying, with (when in Lafferty's last hours the town's mayor asked) a tight smile on his lips. One local legend had it that, from his hatred of the English, Lafferty had planned, after constructing it, to set torch to the town, but that upon seeing it completed, looking upon the beauty of it, as its creator, he could not bring himself to do so.

Some of this I knew from hearsay, Piltdown being a huge tourist draw. The rest I learned from brochures in my motel room and from an hour or two spent with afternoon talkers at the motel bar.

Motel bars at three in the afternoon are bleak, desolate places, deserts for souls turning to stone, where even the light seems somehow *wrong*. This one, after a late-lunchtime rush and a few stragglers-cum-historians, emptied out all at once, leaving only myself, a young blond barkeep wearing a muscle shirt and dwelling in some California of the mind, and, at a table by the crackle-glass front window, the dark lady Shakespeare wrote his sonnets for.

She was reading a newspaper. Every few minutes she'd take a bite out of a sandwich in a serving basket on the table, replace it, and refold the paper to another section. There were also a plastic insulated pitcher of coffee and matching mug.

I drank another beer and watched as she finished sandwich, coffee and paper simultaneously. Then she lifted her head, shook back her hair and looked around. Our eyes met. She smiled.

That hair was so black it seemed to soak up light from the window and leave the rest of the room in shades of gray. Her skin was dark, too—Creole blood, most likely—her eyes a startling blue. She wore a loose-cut white linen suit, pale pink cotton shirt, darker pink tie.

I walked over and introduced myself. Her name was Jeanne—like Baudelaire's dark lady. We moved to a booth and ordered drinks, beer, white wine, from Mr. California.

"Are you staying at the hotel?" she asked.

I said that I was, and returned the question.

"Sort of," she said with a half-second frown. Over her shoulder I watched, on a neon sign, a rainbow of crystal-clear vodka glittering with bright colors arc again and again over the head of a Russian foot soldier who looked remarkably like Maurice Chevalier. "I work here. Again: sort of."

She peered at me, a single huge eye, through the lens of her wine.

"I sing in the club. I'm on the circuit: here one week,

at some other lounge, maybe over in Jackson or Memphis, next week."

"Like it?"

"Beats cutting hair or checking groceries," she said. Then: "I love it. I really do. But the afternoons will simply kill you."

"Some people's lives are *all* afternoons."

She looked at me for a time without saying anything. The vodka rainbow arced over the Russian's head, arced again, a visible heartbeat.

"I don't think I knew that," she said finally. "But you're absolutely right."

She reached over and rested her hand lightly, momentarily, against my own. Her nails were cut short; there was clear polish on them.

"I have to get ready for happy hour. Will you come with me?"

I paid, and we walked out into an assault of sunlight, along a corridor formed by the overhang of the motel's second floor, and around back, where first Dumpsters, then volcanic asphalt, then a stand of oak and evergreen took over.

At her room I waited as she showered. The TV was on with the volume turned low, something old, everything charcoal and silver; she told me she kept it on all the time, for company. I held the beer she'd brought me from a closet-size kitchenette and sat looking around at a toppled stack of books by the bed, fantasy novels mostly; cast-off clothes on the floor in a corner by the bathroom, her guitar case patched with duct tape. It all reminded me uncomfortably of my own life, not so much misspent as somehow misplaced.

Shortly she came out of the bathroom, hair still wet, nipples erect. She held out a hand and I gave her the beer. She drank and handed it back.

"Do you have time to come along? It's only for a couple of hours. We could get dinner or something then, before I start my regular gig at nine. If you want to, that is."

When I said *yes, of course,* it was clear to us both that something far deeper had been decided. Signs again. Hidden meanings, messages. She bent down and kissed me, breasts swaying. One bore a scar, like a twined worm, from nipple to armpit.

She went to the closet and pulled on black jeans, a black sweatshirt, and oversize kelly-green denim shirt. Picked up her guitar case.

"I take requests," she said.

30

Dᴇᴇᴘ ɪɴ ᴛʜᴇ ɴɪɢʜᴛ I woke thinking of Gabrielle.

"Are you okay?" Jeanne said beside me.

"I'm sorry. Restless, I suppose. I didn't mean to wake you."

"It's all right. I don't sleep much anyway."

She got beers from the kitchenette and brought them back to bed. Periodically lights, some dim, others vivid, swept across the back of the room's heavy drapes, as though another world were trying to break through into this one. Traffic was a far-off rumble, like the sea.

She drank, and rolled the cool bottle along the side of her breast, where the scar was.

The room was lit indirectly by the TV screen faced away from us; the flicker of scene changes plucked at the periphery of our vision. Its volume was full off now.

"Are you married?" she said. "Or have you been?"

I shook my head, put my hand on her narrow waist. She covered it with her own.

"Neither have I. I'm thirty-one, and there's so very much I haven't done. I've only seen this one little cluttered corner of the world. I haven't made much effort to understand things that always seemed far beyond my reach, or to become a better human being in any way that matters. Just tread water mostly, tried to stay afloat. I've never loved anyone, or been loved."

"You're an excellent musician, Jeanne. There's tremendous feeling in what you do, every chord or run, the pitch of your voice. And understanding of a sort, too, even if it's intuitive, instinctive, rather than intelligible."

"But that always came easy, like breathing. Or like the way I look: I didn't have much to do with either. I'm attractive, I can play guitar passably and sing. Pretty thin for a biography, and not much of an epitaph. There's one last beer. Split it?"

"I'll go, this time."

We sat quietly drinking, passing the bottle back and forth, and after a while she said, "Two years ago they removed a tumor from my breast. I went to my doctor for a checkup and wound up that same afternoon on the operating table. It was the size of a marble, they said, and benign. There was nothing more to worry about. They'd caught it in time."

After a moment she went on.

"I think sometimes we know things we *can't* know, things that don't make daylight sense, or any sense at all. And we realize how absurd it is for us to believe them. But, still, we know, we just *know.*"

She took my hand in her own and traced the curve of the pale, fine scar along her breast with my finger. The nipple stiffened.

"You're the first man I've been with since then.

Somehow despite whatever they told me, I always knew that when I had a man again, when I finally made love again, the cancer would come back."

She handed me the last of the beer.

"I know how ridiculous this sounds, how crazy it must seem to you. And please don't be frightened. But I can feel it already, like a flower slowly blooming, opening dark petals, inside me.

"Will you make love to me again, David?"

31

We had breakfast and parted. Jeanne had shopping to do, she said, and would be leaving that afternoon for Gulfport and the Holiday Inn there. I sat for a while by the pool. It was nine o'clock, cloudy, and a little like one of those science fiction movies where a few survivors are clinging to the wreckage, living out their days in the dry husk of civilization.

Around front, a chartered Greyhound pulled in. I watched through gaps in the weathered wood fence as twenty or so tourists debarked. All Asian, but a curious mix: Koreans, Thais, a couple of Cambodians, scattered Vietnamese, mainland Chinese in both western and traditional dress. They waited silently in file as the driver went into the motel office and came back out. He stepped along the line, passing keys out.

I didn't think Jeanne's fantasy (if, finally, it *were* fantasy) much stranger than others I've known. We all create such fictions out of the stuff of our lives, small myths, private lies, that help us go on, help us remain human, reassure us that we understand our own tiny fragment of the world. But most of us don't share these myths with strangers. Most of us don't share them at all. And we believe them while knowing at the same time that they *are* fictions.

Maybe that's all my vision of contemplative life, of a life devoted to trying to understand, to the pursuit of balance and beauty, came down to. A private lie, a myth no longer relevant or useful. After all, here I indisputably was. And it was neither balance nor beauty I pursued. The old game, as Holmes said, once again afoot.

I spent the rest of the day afoot as well, treading the streets of Piltdown, in and out of bakeshops and butcher's and haberdasher's and milliner's, from time to time looking off towards the Alabama horizon almost expecting to see thatched-roof cottages there at the town's edge.

Or men with scythes, perhaps, dark against the sun.

32

I FINALLY DROVE, through Montgomery and Mobile, alongside Biloxi and Gulfport and over the rim of Lake Pontchartrain, into New Orleans, arriving there after many hours and one terrible meal tasting indiscriminately of salt, stagnant oil and flour, amazed that Lee Raincrow's decrepit VW had made it here, at three in the morning.

I took the Orleans/Vieux Carre exit off I-10, cut across to Ramparts and down to Esplanade and parked there, in front of a two-story Greek Revival mansion chopped up into half a dozen or so apartments and painted lime green. I walked back up into the Quarter and wandered its narrow streets for a while to unwind. Sidewalks worn smooth and concave like old stone stairs and canting abruptly towards street or stoop. Corner groceries crammed with everything from headache remedies to fifths of Glenlivet to sandwich counters serving up po-boys and muffulettas. Balconies drenched in ferns. Wrought-iron railings, fences and gates behind which you sometimes catch a glimpse of cool, secret inner courtyards. New Orleans is one of the few places in the

States that always feel much the same, year after year—whatever façades they slap up on these century-old buildings, however they jam the streets full of T-shirt and poster shops, massage parlors, fast-food bistros done up in Art Deco or lavender and chrome.

I walked slowly over to Decatur and ambled by the French Market: sharp scent of spices, the deeper earth-smell of rotting fruit and vegetable. Had coffee and beignets at the Café du Monde. Sat by the river watching ships and lights and the long curved spine of the bridge across to the Westbank.

I thought how strange it was to pass directly from Piltdown's antique Oxford to this other ancient place. Something like taking off a coat, turning around and putting it back on. Only in America, as they say.

I thought about assignments and missions and fool's errands.

I thought about those things hard, and for a long time.

Then I walked back to the car, drove uptown to what once had been The Fontainebleu and was now called Fountain Bay (and by the time of my next visit would have become Bayou Plaza), and took a room.

All along Tulane, motels, restaurants and office buildings were boarded up, abandoned. A thrift store had moved into the huge grocer's across Carrollton. Several partially demolished service stations had become used-car lots with six or seven cars, and a proprietor in a folding lawn chair, on them.

"Length of stay?" the desk clerk inquired.

"Undetermined," I told her.

I was given number twelve in The Annex, a string of

cabana-like rooms surrounding the pool inside the motel's larger structure. It was like those old cartoons where a Chaplinesque little man sticks to his rights and remains in his modest house while skyscrapers bloom and sway all about him. It was also like moving to another, uninhabited country. No one else seemed to be booked into The Annex, the city's sounds penetrated hardly at all, and only the sighting of an occasional plane through the rift overhead assured me of the existence of a city, civilization, other living beings more or less like myself.

I hauled in luggage and book bag, showered, and lay on the bed product-testing TV, cable and remote tuner.

Of viable channels, four were showing movies (two mysteries, one horror, one martial arts), another couple were given over to such classics of American culture as "I Love Lucy," "Mister Ed," and "My Favorite Martian," one was all news and public information, three were soaps, and the rest ranged from talk shows with impossibly earnest moderators, to British comedies and Japanese cartoons, to documentaries on the opening of the Panama Canal, prison rodeos and the Harlem Renaissance.

I picked up the phone, called the desk and asked to be connected to room service. After some initial stammering I was put on hold and listened to a lovely rendition of (I think) "Autumn Leaves." Then the music shut off abruptly, as though it had fallen through a trapdoor, and a voice asked if it could help me. I said it could and that I'd like two beers. There was a pause but, mercifully, no more elevator music. Some conversation offstage, or off-mike, as it were. Okay, two beers, the voice finally said. Where do they come? Twelve, I told him. I didn't add: The Annex. By this time I considered the whole thing a bold experiment.

Nevertheless, five minutes later a fiftyish man in jeans and T-shirt showed up at my door with two Millers, a napkin and a chilled glass on a tray. The Easter Bunny wouldn't have been any bigger surprise. I tipped him seriously, poured and, propped with pillows, settled back on the bed, leaving the TV's volume off, watching from some far-off place the rush of images across its screen.

I thought back to all my years in and out of the country, in a kind of exile really, when I was able to look back on the States for long periods of time as an outsider, gathering my knowledge of its affairs from French- and Spanish-language newspapers, local (wherever local happened to be) radio and television, rumor, armed-service broadcasts and the BBC. I'd known a different America then. Maybe it *was* a different America.

Assignments and missions and fool's errands.

Lights were on all over town, Johnsson had said.

No more Cold War, no Big Bad Bear. When society has no further need of the warriors it has created, do *they* perhaps come to be perceived as a threat? Does that society come to believe that it must reject them, isolate them, find some way to set them against one another?

Were there others still at my back?

I'd seen no signs of such purposeful companionship since that young man's death. Johnsson had seemed to think it was all over, my dance card filled. Yet he had also voiced concern for Gabrielle's safety.

1. Maybe Michael was just who and what he claimed, and it *was* all over.

2. Maybe Planchat (as Johnsson believed) was dead and out of the picture.

3. Maybe one, or two, or ten other soldiers were even now snuffling across Lake Pontchartrain into New Orleans, hot on my trail.

4. Maybe they were sent out, assigned, only to shadow me, to see where I, or whoever else was dogging me, or whoever I in turn was dogging, would lead them.

5. Maybe, like my shadow self back in that Memphis motel room, they were assassins-in-waiting.

6. Maybe none of the above.

7. Maybe all of the above.

33

THE AGENCY'S LANGUAGE school was as unorthodox, as given to getting things done by whatever necessary means, as the agency itself. When I went through, for many years afterwards in the flesh, and forever in spirit, the school consisted of Rima Palangian. Like Cohen with his theories of clothing, in another of those odd dislocations common to the era, Rima had been recruited from academia. Born of a Polish father and Russian mother, she'd once been the highest-paid translator in Moscow. In the early seventies she tired of walking her tightrope and, on holiday at a conference in Rome, requested entry to the U.S. Major American universities leapt from the water. She chose Princeton, and a couple of years later the agency chose her.

With Chomsky, and flying in the face of standard American adherence to Sapir-Whorf, Rima believed language to be encoded genetically within us. And so there were no formal classes: no memorization of vocabulary, no conjugation drills, no lengthy diagrams or descriptions of grammar. Instead, Rima showed foreign-language films and advertisements, tuned in to European broadcasts via satellite linkages, strode among us speaking full tilt in various languages, often switching from one to another in midsentence.

And she gave us poetry.

Pavese, for instance, when we "studied" (lived in) Italian. Rilke and Günter Grass for German. Mandelstam. Li Po. Neruda.

But, first of all: Apollinaire.

She was especially fond of Apollinaire, whose mother was Polish, father a mystery. He had revolutionized French poetry, hauling it by its bootstraps into the modern era. He had gone off to war and come back with a steel plate in his head. Trepanning, they called it: opening a window in the poet's pear-shaped skull to relieve pressure.

Rima would chant these poems again and again until, though we had little if any idea of their meaning, their sounds had become a part of us, mingled somehow with our own heartbeats, with our breath. And finally, suddenly, we'd reach a point where we knew, or at least *felt,* what the poems were about: what was happening in them, what they had to tell us. One moment the poem was there, an object, a sound, a cadence outside you; the next, it was within, curtains pulling back at window after window along the street. A whole new world.

With me, I'll never forget, it was a poem called "Cors de chasse."

Notre histoire est noble et tragique

Passons passons puisque tout passe
Je me retournerai souvent

Rima had spent the morning in a discussion of current affairs in Europe, in French, of course, returning every few minutes to the poem, chanting it several times, going back to current affairs. On the ninth or tenth repetition, realizing that I knew what the poem said—and that now I could follow, as well, *most* of what she was saying—I looked up. It was an amazing moment; there have been few like it in my life.

> *Memory is a hunting horn*
> *It dies along the wind*

Rima was watching me closely. She smiled, nodded, and went on with her teaching.

La vie, she'd always say, breaking the back of syntax and common usage, *c'est toujours entre.* Life is always *in between.* Life was what happened while you were waiting around for *other* things to happen. Life was what sprang up in the places you never thought to look. *In between.*

Like the things we learn, truly learn, I know now, from the few true teachers we have in our lives.

34

I SLEPT TILL LATE afternoon, woke thinking of Gabrielle, then, more an anamnesis, an unfolding, than simple memory, recalled the dream.

Seeking a wise man reputed to live here, I moved ever deeper, through narrow, branching tunnels, into a cave. The cave's entrance was at the edge of a golf course encircled by ancient oaks whose limbs spidered out as much as twenty feet; some from sheer weight had gone back to ground, as though to root there anew. Vague impressions of a city skyline, of gray stone buildings, of a bell tower looming above trees, trailed behind me as I entered the cave, leaving light behind.

Descending, I passed though discrete strata of sound as well: traffic noise from streets bordering the park, the spin and whirr of bikes and rollerblades and the measured footfall of runners, the call of ducks and geese from the central lagoon.

Orderly blocks of writing in some unknown language, looking to be a mixture of cuneiform and script, covered the walls of one passageway. Touched, it came off on my hand, like newsprint or transfer tattoos.

Once, entering a chamber, I saw what I was certain was the cave's inhabitant, the wise man, moving towards another tunnel to elude me—but it was only a rock formation, an excrescence of salts.

I could hear my own blood rushing in my ears, as though heavy winds blew through the cave, as though all about me things were being said that I couldn't make out.

Around another bend I came upon a mass that blocked my way: a root system, I realized, all but filling the chamber, pursuing its own life down here, a life little concerned with that of the tree above. Dark, formless birds perched on its knuckles and knees.

I made my way past them and weaved through tooth-like crystalline formations above and below. Then emerged from one of the cave's many throats into another open space where, suddenly, light struck with the force of a physical blow and, reeling, half-blind, I found myself again outside, standing at the base of one of the massive oaks.

I looked up. High on its trunk a small brass plaque bore, both in Latin and in English, the tree's genus and species. The plaque was badly weathered and tarnished; a glare of sunlight further obscured it to the point that I was unable to make it out. I woke still trying.

But I knew those plaques and implacable oaks, knew where I had been in the dream.

New Orleans.

Audubon Park.

Back in Sheriff Pickett's office I hadn't known that New Orleans was my destination until I said it. And even then, I didn't know why.

Now the dream was trying to push through, to tell me something.

All those turns and branchings, all that darkness and disorientation, the search for a wise man, *gathering intelligence* as they say—these were my wayward, blind trip down from Washington.

And knowing that, I suddenly knew, as well, that Gabrielle was the reason I'd made my way, however circuitously and circumspectly, to New Orleans. It had little or nothing to do with Planchat and whatever others were out there. Gabrielle had family here: I remembered now. Somehow intuition had guided me. Somehow I had known, intuited, suspected, that Gabrielle would become important to the end of this affair, that I would need to find her.

I pulled on jeans, T-shirt and boots and walked across Tulane to a pay phone outside the Genghis Khan.

Johnsson himself answered.

"Checking in, sir."

"Ah: David. We thought perhaps you had seen fit to leave us again."

When I said nothing, he went on.

"Things have been peculiarly quiet at this end."

"Here, too."

"Though all the lights, insofar as we're able to ascertain, remain on." He was silent a moment. "You are well?"

"Yes."

Another pause. "And your plans?"

"What I believe you once called 'creative waiting.'"

"Yes, I did say that, didn't I? In another time, one that seems far away now. Is it possible that the world has truly passed us so terribly by, David? That all the things we cared for so passionately, all the things we believed so strongly, have come to be of no more consequence than an old sweater, a stamp collection?"

"I suspect *all* our passions are mere stamp collections to those who don't share them."

"Yes. You're almost certainly right." He turned away, coughed. "May we expect you to check in at regular intervals, then?"

"Yes, sir."

"And if there is anything you need, you will let us know, let *me* know, at once."

"I will."

"I wish there were more I could do. I was not meant for these new games, David."

"None of us were."

"Take care, then."

I was about to hang up when he said: "David."

"Yes."

"One other thing. I had not intended to tell you this, but you will want to know. Blaise is missing."

"Missing?"

"He was last seen during a routine room check two nights ago. When the nursing assistant went in the next morning to get everyone up, he was gone. His bed, seemingly, had not been slept in. His wallet, a small suitcase and select clothing were also missing."

"How much money could he have had squirreled away there?"

"Not much, according to the doctors. Not that it matters. *You* never had much trouble getting money when you needed it. None of you did."

"Any notion at all where he might be?"

"Quite frankly, I can't imagine Blaise going anywhere but right back here. He had no family, no friends or particular place. The agency's *been* his life."

"No sign of violence, I take it."

"None. There does seem to be a car, a Plymouth Reliant belonging to the night orderly, also missing."

"He broke out."

"That is our assumption, yes. Though of course we have a number of men pursuing every possible lead. I'll keep you abreast, naturally."

We listened for a moment to the line sweepers.

"Thank you, sir," I said, and hung up.

I walked back across Tulane to my room, stripped and showered. Then, still wet, I lay on the bed thinking about Blaise, about Gabrielle, about the kid who had died out there on the service road—Adrian?

I decided that I needed, in approximate order: food, people and music.

The first is always easy to take care of in New Orleans, where even rat-hole cafés and corner groceries are likely to have some of the best food you'll eat. Both the other items on my list, I found at a Cajun-music bar in the warehouse district.

Actually it was more of a dance hall: a vast, long room with picnic tables along the periphery, at one end some sagging flats stacked for a stage, at the other a door to the kitchen with a window alongside through which you could order drinks. But the sign outside said BAR. And that's *all* it said.

The fiddler looked like something carved from hardwood and left out in years of bad weather; his hair was the wavy, peaked kind you see in forties photos, still jet black. The accordionist was younger, early thirties, with longish hair and a red sport jacket, sleeves pushed up, over a Jazzfest T-shirt and black jeans. The guitarist fronted for the band and sang, working in five or six jokes Hannibal probably told his troops. The bass player picked and slapped at his instrument as though he were somewhere else far away watching all this.

I pushed into BAR through tides of smoke, a gaggle of children and the sound of "La Porte dans Arriére." Most of the audience joined in to shout out the repeating last line of each verse.

A dozen or so older children sat at a corner table, some of them over card or computer games, one reading a Dr. Seuss book in French. Women swept about with plates and bowls of food—*boudin,* red beans, jambalaya and gumbo, fried catfish—or with mugs of thick chicory coffee and hot milk.

I grabbed a beer, an Abita, at the window and sat at one of the tables. Cajun music was what I needed just now. The band threw in something country every third or fourth number, Hank Williams mostly, but these songs came out sounding much like the rest, even the familiar lyrics bent and clipped to strangeness.

A baby crawled beneath my table, pursuing a rattle that rolled away whenever it was touched. A young couple who'd been dancing every song finally quit the floor and went outside, probably to hose themselves down.

With a long warble from the accordion, the band struck into an achingly slow "J'ai Passé Devant Ta Porte."

I walked by your door and cried bye-bye. There was no one to answer; my heart was sick. When I knocked at the door, when they let me in, I saw the bright candles all around your casket.

That's all: two verses. And a waltz. Only Cajuns would make a waltz of something like that.

Having tugged every possible sob from the fiddle, having wrenched from the accordion one final wracking sigh, the band hove without warning into a headlong instrumental before taking its break.

I drank, listened to music and watched dancers through another hour-long set and another break, then left BAR for streets so humid that lights were shelled in hazy rainbows and every window ran with condensation.

Getting into Lee Raincrow's VW on Julia, still amazed the thing was running at all, I glanced up and thought I saw someone pull back into the dark of a doorway.

As I parked on Tulane half a block down from Fountain Bay, I caught a glimpse of a face looking out from a passing car, turning quickly away.

35

I<small>N THE DREAM</small>, largely a new edition of last night's (itself transformed, translated, transmogrified), everything was change. Trees became huge shadowy spiders shouldering towards me through the landscape; or the twisted fingers and arms of old men urging me on towards knowledge and confrontations I didn't care to have. Then, without warning or transition, they were snugly furnished, carpeted rooms where I sat talking with Johnsson, Gabrielle, Planchat, Blaise. Then, like trapdoors dropping open, tunnels down which I tumbled to the very center of the earth. Lava rose towards me in the trunk as I fell, fell again, went on falling forever. If only I made it through the lava somehow, at earth's center there'd be no gravity, no air: there I'd be weightless, free; wouldn't need even to breathe.

The phone's ringing woke me, and I floundered, out of breath, still in a panic, on the bed. When I picked the phone up there was no answer.

Then suddenly it was as if I were awakened again—or was this the same time, only seconds later, perhaps? I had thought the phone to be ringing. But the phone was silent. Had I dreamed its earlier ringing? Or had it actually rung then, had I spoken into it? And just now? I tried for a time to remember some telling detail that might assure me—light at the window as I first awoke, sounds from outside my room, the feel of tangled sheets beneath me or my feet on the room's rough carpet—before finally giving up.

Cut to the chase, then. Or more accurately, after coffee and rolls at La Madeleine, to the search.

New Orleans has expansive Irish and Latin populations. They don't live in discrete communities, as they would elsewhere, but scattered about here and there throughout the city's semidetached neighborhoods.

Gabrielle would have gone to ground near family in one or the other of those populations. I decided to take a chance on the luck of the Irish, and after trying Kelly's Pub out on Airline and Mickey F's Bar downtown, wound up at O'Toole's.

O'TOOLE'S has been IN THE SAME LOCATION (moving one building up Magazine towards Louisiana when the original bar burned out in the fifties, and around the corner, into an old auction house, in the seventies when antique stores moved in along that part of Magazine and property values doubled overnight) FOR 86 YEARS.

Some of the tables and chairs and decorations hung on the wall looked to have been here the whole time. So did a couple sitting at the bar.

I sat beside them and introduced myself, offering to buy them a drink if they'd like.

The man turned his head and looked at me a moment.

"Mary," he said. He tilted his head half an inch back towards his companion. Then, turning away, looking straight ahead again: "Patrick." A pause. "Sheehy. We'd be pleased enough to drink a beer with you, sir."

Actually, they were pleased enough to drink three with me. Possibly four. They also filled me in on the bar's history.

I described Gabrielle and asked if they'd seen her.

They looked briefly at one another.

"She's here in N'Orleans, you say?" the man said.

"I think so. Yes, sir."

"Black hair. Irish, and with a Spanish accent."

"It comes and goes, but yes."

"Well. There couldn't be many like that walking about, even here, could there be?"

"No, sir."

"And would she be wantin' to see *you,* d'you think, young man?"

I told him a version of the truth. That a job had taken me away from her. That she had written she'd be waiting for me. That we were in love.

When I was through, he looked at his wife.

"John Neil?" he said.

She nodded, that same half-inch.

He looked back to me.

"A nephew of ours manages rental properties about town. Owns a fair portion of it himself, oversees the rest for others. He just might be able to help you find your young lady."

He lifted a paper coaster from a stack of them on the bar, turned it over and scribbled an address.

"You'll be wantin' the little house out back, not the one facin' on the street. Go 'round to the right, and there'll be a gate set in just a bit, with a brick path back to the little house. That's where John Neil lives. Rents out the big house."

I thanked him.

"I know things're some different now, young man. But if I were you, when I did find my young lady, I'd be sure to take along a nice bunch of flowers."

He glanced at his wife. She smiled at him.

"Maybe two bunches," he said.

In Louisiana there's an animal called the nutria. Think of a cross between a beaver and a hamster the size of a small dog, and you pretty much have it. John Neil Noel's mother, as they say, had been frightened by one. He stood on hind legs, but the resemblance otherwise, from body shape and the layer of soft dark hair visible on every exposed body part, to fitful, quick movements, was uncanny.

"Mm-hm," Noel said. His pointed face went sharply from left to right, darted towards my own, the window, the floor. "Hmmmm."

On my way there, I'd stopped by a Kwik-Kopy on St. Charles and faxed a coded request to Johnsson at one of the agency's blinds. Within fifteen minutes a clerk had gone electronically calling at the Department of Motor Vehicles, obtained a copy of Gabrielle's driver's license photo, and faxed it back to me.

I showed the photo to Noel now, eliciting another "Hmmmm."

"I think," he said. Looked away. "Pretty sure, really." Looking back. "Yeah. Property down on Camp, just off Melpomene."

"How long has she been there?"

"Week, maybe."

"Alone?"

"You bet. Place's too small for more'n one. Walk in frontways, you gotta back back out when you leave. Hard to rent 'cause of it."

"Lease?"

"Monthly. Six units to the building. Four of 'em, the owner's got long-term tenants, been with him for years. But there's two more tacked onto the back, and those, he lets month to month."

"You're sure it's her?"

"She got a twin? A whatsit. Doppelgänger?"

I shook my head.

"Then it's gotta be her."

He opened a drawer of the desk, took out a business card, wrote an address on the back.

"You hold on to this card once you're done with it, now. Be back here someday needing a place to stay, you'll know where to come."

I drove down Prytania to Terpsichore and across to Coliseum, then curved around the knothole-shaped park, turned onto Race and, a block over, hit Camp.

Set close to the street, the disheveled Victorian house had seen many colors over the years; recently it had been oversprayed with a thin coat of white. There was a sidewalk once, and an iron fence, but the roots of a huge oak had heaved up through the former and shattered it, leaving only some fragments of concrete at the yard's edge, and the remaining couple of feet of fence, driven by those same roots, all but protruded from the ground at a forty-degree angle to it. The oak loomed above the house and stretched one long crooked arm out over the street, but it was dying now.

I followed a narrow path that curved beneath ten-foot banana trees and through thick hedges gone native, to the back of the house. The path's bricks were flush with the ground, many in fact recessed, and streamers of grass and weed grew through them all; those at the edge were worn smooth.

The apartment's door stood ajar. A window, too, was open, and a blue curtain rippled in and out of it, flaglike.

I stood stock still, listening.

Shouts from back in the park. Cars easing their way over pitted streets nearby. The bleat of a house alarm off towards Prytania.

I went slowly up to the door and again stood listening. A radio or TV was on inside, in the back room, volume turned low. Nothing else to be heard. I slipped over the sill and was in.

There were only the two rooms, with a tiny kitchen tucked away at one front corner and an even tinier bathroom at the opposite back corner. Furnished sparsely and simply—a wicker love seat, a couple of straight-back chairs, a low table—the front room was as orderly and unlived-in-looking as a motel room, yet managed, for all that, somehow to feel cozy. Foodstuffs and utensils neatly lined kitchen shelves. Clean dishes lay in a draining rack over the sink.

The back room was another story.

Here, a hurricane touched down.

Sheets and cotton blankets had been torn away from the bed and left in drifts on the floor nearby. Cosmetics, perfumes, mirrors and brushes from atop the bureau lay scattered about. A wooden chair knelt forward onto broken front legs. Capsized at the end of its taut cord, the TV cast its dim searchlight at the ceiling.

My foot nudged a music box lying on its side. Two or three notes came reluctantly out.

Bending, I pushed sheet and blanket away from a corner of something and picked it up.

Its cover showed a young man in glasses, serious as only the young *can* be, something of an intellectual, surely, but with sensuous lips and a far-off, dreamy look to his eyes behind the steel rims. Beyond, sketchy olive trees and open fields stretched to the horizon and what might with equal likelihood be clouds or encroaching city.

Poems of Cesare Pavese.

36

"I TOLDJA SOMETHING bad was going on over there."

Square in the doorway, she still looked ahead, at me, but clearly her remark was addressed to someone in the room beyond. She wore stretch pants gone baggy at buttock and knee, a matching loose pullover aglitter with metallic threads and sequins. Her hair, crisped by decades of chemicals, was ambiguously mahogany, black, grayish-green.

A younger man stepped up behind her, drink in hand. High cheekbones of an Indian, Latinate bronze skin. His head rolled along her shoulder as he looked me over. He nodded, possibly in greeting, possibly in confirmation of everything he'd suspected, and withdrew.

"Could you tell me what you saw, Ms. . . . ?"

"Cohen. And it's Mrs. But everyone just calls me Irene."

I waited, but we seemed to have lost the thread somewhere, the train become derailed.

"What you saw," I prompted. Then: "Irene."

It was as though a switch, a relay, had clicked on.

"I was doing dishes. Quite a stack of 'em since Al ain't

been feeling too good and I've been working all the hours I could get at the shop and ain't either of us been able to get around to dishes for a while. Window over the sink looks out on them apartments back there. There's all sorts that come and go back there, have for years. Some days it's as good a show as you're gonna find anywhere in town."

She glanced over my shoulder. At the open door there across the alleyway, the blue curtain waving in the window.

"Two men come to the door. It was open just like it is now. Usually was—no air conditioning, you know? They had on suits, which ain't something you see a lot of 'round here, so naturally I know they got to be law of some kind, right? They knock on the door and when she comes to it the three of them stand there in the doorway talking a little, and then the one doing most of the talking just kind of pushes her on back in the room. The other one looks around him a minute, then he goes in too."

"You see or hear anything else?"

"Not till they come back out I didn't."

"How long was that?"

"Ten, fifteen minutes maybe. I'd finished the dishes by then. Al and I was taking the dog over by the park to do his thing. You know. So we're coming around the corner onto Camp and see these guys in suits coming out from behind the house with the woman."

"This one."

She looked at the photo.

"Could be her, yeah."

"Did she appear to be struggling?"

"Not that you could tell. They was holding on to her arms, though, I'm pretty sure. One on each side. They got in a car, her and the guy who done the talking in back, the other guy in front, and drove off."

"On up Camp? To the bridge ramp?"

She shook her head. "Turned back towards the river."

"Do you remember what kind of car they were in, Irene?"

"Couldn't tell you. Never drove one, don't know a Ford from a John Deere."

"Light or dark?"

"Oh, it was dark. Blue, almost black."

"Was it a compact—a small car—or full size?"

She thought about it.

"Four doors, or just two?" I prompted.

"Oh, it had four. And it was big, like the law drives."

"Thanks, Irene. You've been a great help."

I had turned to go when she said, "You don't want to know about the other car, then?"

I looked back at her.

"As they were pulling away, a man stepped out from between houses. He got in a car parked down the street a ways and, near as I could tell, took out after them. Turned that same way, anyhow, and by then he was going a fair clip."

"Did you get a good look at him?"

"Afraid not. Too far off for me. Don't think he was a *young* man, though, like those others. Moved more like me or Al, you know?"

"Could you tell how he was dressed?"

"Just pants, what they call slacks, I guess, light-colored. And a golf jacket kind of thing, a windbreaker.

Dark shirt under it. One of them athletic shirts, I think."

"And his car?"

"Blue."

"Dark blue, or light?"

"Light."

"Size?"

"Not as big as the other one, but not like those little foreign jobs either. The ones that look like lunchboxes."

"Two doors?"

She shrugged. "I guess."

"Anything else?"

She thought about it. "Unh-unh."

I thanked her and turned again to go.

Al's voice came from the room behind her.

"First car was a Continental, royal blue, '90 or '91. Rear axle's bad on it, and the cylinders are dirty. Other guy had him a Plymouth. Reliant, I think they call it. Nothing wrong with that one. Someone took good care of it. Body's some banged up, but hey, who cares? It's solid. Sound."

I peered around the door. Al raised his drink to me.

"Man's as fine a mechanic as you'll find anywhere," the woman said. "Or used to be anyhow, when he was able to work. Had a true gift. Lots of people said it, and they brought their cars to him from all over. I guess cars is the only thing he ever loved."

She turned briefly away. The smile came back around with her. Her whole face had changed.

" 'Cept me, of course."

37

OVERSEXED AND EVER-RAVENOUS, nutria are virtually devouring the state's coastline, while both New Orleans and Louisiana politicians do *their* time-honored best to devour the rest.

Huey Long taught people down here a lot of things: every pot ought to have a chicken in it, every man was a king, no man should wear a crown. Probably the most enduring thing he taught (in those pre-Camelot days) was that a strong man could always go *around,* get things done *his* way. And it's been free-style, catch-as-catch-can politics in Louisiana ever since.

All of it confusing as hell, true—a constant, continuous upheaval for residents, absolutely impenetrable to everyone else—but there's no better place for calling in favors. Favors are understood in a big way down around New Orleans. And Johnsson's fifty-odd years in government added up to a hell of a lot of favors.

Networking, they call it now.

Yeah, I know all about fierce American individualism and independence. Natty Bumppo, mountain men, Thoreau, Huck Finn, cowboys, utopian communities,

Chandler's dark knight, Holden Caulfield, hippies. Head out on the highway. Do your own thing. Go west till you've used that up, too. Just say no—like Bartleby. Just do it.

And I revere all that.

Nevertheless, half an hour later I had half a dozen parish and state agencies, the state police and every squad car in New Orleans on my dance card.

The Sikhs, for all their spiritualism, may be right: if you're poor, you're stupid. And if information's the currency of the day and you have access to it and don't use it, then *you're* stupid.

A call to Johnsson was all it took. He rang up a few senators and department heads, a committee chairman or two, and it started trickling down fast. Royal-blue Lincolns and Plymouth Reliants were being checked out all over: Algiers, Chalmette, LaPlace, Shreveport, even on into Mississippi and Alabama.

I sat in my hotel room fielding calls. The sixth one from NOPD shut it all down.

A Lincoln answering to my description was known to frequent a strip shopping center on Tchoupitoulas. Area patrols began noticing it after several ticketings for irregular parking; subsequently there'd been a minor collision involving the car, no real damage or injury, the incident dutifully reported by the other car's driver at time of occurrence.

It was like the click Emily Dickinson talked about, when she knew she had a poem. Or like Housman, who'd recite prospective lines while shaving in the morning, and when his beard hairs went on end, then he knew he had it.

That Lincoln felt like the shell my pea was under.

I took St. Charles up to Jefferson, then Jefferson towards the river till it dead-ended into Tchoupitoulas. The Continental was parked around the corner from Alfalfa Video, on a side street, well back from the intersection and from fire hydrants.

I pulled in behind and got out. Squatted for a close look. Both rear tires were worn badly on the inside.

The surrounding houses were shotgun doubles, set a couple of feet off the ground, with roofs that overhung narrow porches—galleries, they call them here. Potted plants crowded the nearest one: that didn't seem likely. Kids played on Big Wheels and plastic bikes before another across the street. An elderly black couple sat in lawn chairs on the gallery adjoining.

But next down, the gallery was bare, floorboards and steps showing little sign of use. Miniblinds lidded both front windows. A band of pink impatiens bordered the brick walkway. Grass in the door-size front yard had been clipped to a uniform half-inch and carefully edged at flowerbed, sidewalk, walkway.

I knocked, and a face canted out from behind the door as it opened. The face's black chevron of a monobrow tensed at its center.

"Yeah?"

"I apologize for disturbing you in your home," I said.

"Yeah?" Same intonation.

"Mind your manners now," came a voice from within. "Ask our visitor to step in, why don't you?"

Monobrow backed out of the doorway. I took a couple of steps. Behind him were two enforcers—bonebreakers, as they're called. Six-foot-two, two-forty or so, thighs and necks like tree trunks. Lots of good home cooking Sicilian style. Mind you, they didn't look too dangerous just now, what with the duct tape holding them in their chairs and the socks stuffed in their mouths.

Blaise sat on a straight-back chair with ovals of quilted padding at seat and back. Beside him on a spindly oval-topped table sat a cup and saucer and, as though it were just another common tea utensil, a small pistol, a Glock.

"David," Blaise said. "I had a feeling you might be along shortly. If I'd been certain, I might have saved myself the trip. *Not* that I had anything better to do, you understand."

He glanced at Monobrow, and nodded towards an armchair. Monobrow, who looked like a larval version of the other two, pale and somehow unformed, quickly sat. Vinyl creaked beneath him.

"Thank you," Blaise said. He nodded at the enforcers. "I've never much cared for gagging a man. But these two insisted upon raising such a ruckus when they came around, they left me no choice."

He smiled.

"Good to see you again, David." He sipped tea from the cup beside him and set it precisely back into the saucer's concavity. "Outstanding tea, young man. *Mes compliments.*"

"Name's Donny," Monobrow said. "And fuck you, you old fart."

Blaise sighed. "They never get it, do they? The new generation. Remember when you only ran into professionals out here? Now you got kids who learned their trade from cop shows on TV. I still remember something you once told me. 'In America, each new generation is a new people.' "

"Gertrude Stein: I remember. I also remember that the last time I saw you, you couldn't talk."

"Yes. Well: things change, don't they?"

He glanced again at the two bone-breakers, at Monobrow.

"You have any idea who these jokers are?"

I shook my head. "Seem to be an awful lot of chickens loose in the yard. All of them pecking away at all the others."

"The night I left, I woke up thinking you shouldn't be out here alone. And before I knew it, I'd said it out loud there in the room. Sound of my own voice scared the hell out of me. Also made me realize I was right, and I started packing." He laughed. "Now I see I needn't have worried: you weren't alone at all. All *kinds* of company. These three aren't players, though. Strictly subcontractors, work for hire. We've talked things over, and they assure me they're off the case."

Blaise nodded to a door at his left.

"She's in there. Sleeping. She's fine. *That's* what I was most concerned about."

38

ONCE NEW ORLEANS (Blaise told me as I saw Gabrielle
and him off to their plane) had been a walled city. In place
almost from the beginning, walls and forts endured for
over a hundred years, though never in all that time were
they of use in repelling attackers.

French maps as early as 1725 show a surrounding wall
with small forts. Four years later following the Natchez
Massacre, with New Orleanians thinking they might well
be the next target of Indian attacks, a palisade flanked by
a moat and small blockhouses with artillery went up.
French Governor Luis Billouart de Kerlerec reported his
restoration of these fortifications to the king; though
when Louisiana passed into Spanish hands in 1762 and
Governor Bernardo de Gálvez (who would become a
hero of the Revolutionary War, driving the British sum-
marily from the state) evaluated the fortifications, he
found them laughable.

It was Governor Carondelet who, in 1794, consoli-
dated these walls and forts. His predecessor had been run
out of Louisiana by citizens who, though under Spanish
rule, still considered themselves Frenchmen *au coeur,* and

Carondelet was determined not to let things get out of hand. The fact that heads were rolling back in France, literally, helped support his resolve. That sort of thing might easily spread to the new world.

And so each of Governor Carondelet's days began with a tour of the fifteen-foot wall of mud going up at the city's perimeter, soon to be topped with palisades and fronted by a forty-foot moat. At the river, twenty feet high and studded with cannon, two pentagonal forts were erected: Fort St. Louis (at Canal Street) and Fort St. Charles (at Esplanade). Three additional forts protected the city's rear.

Facing the river, Forts St. Louis and St. Charles were far the most formidable. Yet from the first, walls and forts alike had been built as much to keep the French in, to keep them in every sense contained, as to repel outside forces.

By the time of Louisiana's sale to America in 1803, wall and forts were again crumbling. William Claiborne, the first American governor, reported that final demolition was made easier when on a dark night one of the rear forts was stolen in its entirety, presumably for use as firewood.

39

"THE WORLD HAS changed more than we can imagine, David," Blaise said.

Outside, a midsize plane painted white with blue stripes that ran its length, looking like seersucker, breasted into the sky.

"Or perhaps it's only that, having changed ourselves, we can no longer see it as we once did."

We hunched over our coffees. They'd come out of a machine the size of a small refrigerator that promised to deliver everything from espresso and cappuccino to hot chocolate and local café au lait. I, for one, had my doubts. I'd seen the counterman emptying in bags of powder as we approached, before he turned to serve us.

To our right, passengers with camera cases and back-packs emerged from International Arrivals. To our left, huge Mardi Gras masks, gold, green and purple, a clown, a witch, a lion, loomed above an exit.

Gabrielle came back from the rest room. I pushed a questionable *au lait* in its Styrofoam cup towards her.

"Good luck," I said.

She sniffed at it, looked into the container as though

wondering when the goldfish might have died.

"So much for New Orleans's reputation."

"You're in Jefferson Parish now, honey child. Out here on the frontier, it's every man for himself."

"What about the women?"

"They're for himself too."

"Figures." She turned to Blaise. "I overheard what you were just saying, the last part anyhow. You think people ever really change? In any way that matters, that makes a difference?"

"Well . . . You come right down to it, I guess I have to, chère."

A gaggle of middle-aged Germans came out of the corridor from International Arrivals. The guard at the gate said something to them in German. Keeping faces averted into their own group, they responded, laughing.

"What about those?"

Gabrielle nodded towards a dozen young Latin males in muscle shirts and white slacks. They were seated in a line, matching blue athletic bags at each of their feet.

"You think I should go over and tell them that their women will be making their own decisions from now on?"

"Good point," Blaise said. "But what about him?" nodding towards me.

"Well, true, he's a special case. Always has been."

"*He's* changed."

"More than I wanted to, originally," I said. "And far *less* than I wanted to ultimately."

Blaise's eyes followed another plane heaving itself into sky. "Life is so very peculiar. So *particular*," he said. "Like a series of snapshots, each one of them slightly, all but imperceptibly, different from the one before. But, still, by the end of the series *everything* is different. You look up and don't know where you are anymore; it might just as well be another world."

"Maybe it *is* another world. Johnsson told me that all the things we cared for so passionately, all the things we believed so strongly, were gone now. That they'd come to be of no more consequence than an old sweater, or a stamp collection."

"Johnsson admitted that?"

I nodded.

"Amazing. And I've known the man, worked with him, over forty years."

I shrugged.

"He is rather a walled city, himself, you know. I suppose we all have been. The nature of the beast, eh, David?"

"Of walls, at least. And Joshua out there now with his trumpet."

"Perhaps so."

"There's a poem by Cavafy, a Greek, that I've been thinking about a lot, Blaise. 'The Barbarians.' In it, this city's always gearing up for imminent attack. People working together, making decisions and passing laws, gathering foodstuffs, building, arming themselves. Because soon the barbarians will be at the gates. And this has been going on for years, for lifetimes. But the barbarians never come, and finally people realize they aren't *going* to come, and then everything begins to fall apart. The poet says he doesn't know what they'll do now without the barbarians. Those people, he writes, were a kind of solution."

Blaise put his empty cup on the table by my own. Gabrielle's remained full.

"It seems there are still barbarians at *your* walls, David."

"Whatever far land they come from, and to whatever purpose: yes. But not a tribe, perhaps. Maybe only a single wild man."

"You know that Gabrielle will be kept safe?"

"Yes. And I thank you."

"Even you won't know where we are. But when it's over—I will know when it's over—I'll bring her to you."

I nodded.

"I don't understand this," he said.

"Nor do I."

"But I don't *have* to understand."

He stood. "Our plane should be about to board." He held out his hand. We shook, then embraced. "What will you do now, my friend?"

"Be still, I suppose, and silent, and trust this may bring them in closer to me."

"You will be wanting a moment alone," he said, and stepped off towards the concourse.

"Blaise."

He stopped. "Yes?"

"You understand why I never came back."

"Ah. But David: you did."

He turned away again, into the concourse, the crowd.

"He's a wonderful man," Gabrielle said.

"He is."

"I only wish I could have known about him before this, known how important he was to you."

"I—"

"No. I'm not asking for explanations, David. *I* don't have to understand, either. But that doesn't mean I don't want to. That I don't hope, in the future, all this might become a part of my life, too."

"How could you want it to?"

"I don't even know what *it* is, not really. But I know who you are. And *it* is part of you. A larger part than you want to admit."

She leaned into me. My arms went around her.

"I love you," she said.

"Yes. You do."

Then she and Blaise were walking away towards the gates.

I hurried to the escalator and stood at a railing high over the concourse watching them make their way together across the polished floor. Line after line of travelers with wrapped bundles and luggage—golf clubs, guitar cases, shopping bags, matched leather—milled at ticket counters right and left. Blaise and Gabrielle walked through them all, down the floor's empty center, into sunlight.

When they were out of sight I retrieved the car from level A-4 (yep, still running, still indomitable) and drove back down Airline, past dozens of makeshift businesses and ramshackle motels advertising free movies and weekly rates, to the hotel. I showered and shaved, and walked across Tulane for breakfast at the Home Plate Inn. It was what used to be called a luncheonette. Huge letters high on the front window announced WE NEVER CLOSE. There was little window space left among a jumble of legends such as *Po-Boys, Daily Specials, Steaks,*

Breakfast Any Time, and what space there was, bore a grayish-brown film of forty years' grease, smoke and bad city air, like geological strata. But the eggs, grits and biscuits were first rate.

So was the coffee, and I walked another large black back to my room. I lay for a while propped on the bed, idly browsing TV—a piece on Japanese gardens, a profile of Anna Akhmatova I'd seen before, a Jerry Lewis movie, various sports events, news updates, cooking shows—thinking about Gabrielle, about Blaise, about Adrian's death there on that service road. Then I discovered an FM-radio channel playing Mahler's First and put the remote down.

Sometime during the second movement's achingly slow minor-key version of "Frère Jacques," I fell asleep.

When I awoke the next morning, Luc Planchat was sitting beside the bed drinking coffee from a plastic cup.

40

He put another like it on the table beside me. The lamp's round, frosted globe hung above it like a sun gone cold. Morning light held its breath, oddly depthless, oddly indeterminate, in the window.

"Au lait," he said. "Fresh. And," retrieving a waxed-paper bag from the floor by his chair, "hot, or at least still warm, I hope, beignets."

I pried off the cup's lid and let steam come up around my face. It smelled of nuts and fecund earth and growing things, its depth and richness for a moment pre-empting the world's glib surface. I took a sip. The taste wasn't as rich as the smell—what actuality ever fulfills anticipation?—but it was close enough.

We sat there. Indistinct voices passed by in the hallway. Sunlight swarmed at the window behind blinds and deadfall drapes, rummaging for entry at some corner, quarter or edge, seeking recognition.

"I know your work, old friend," Planchat said. "I'm a fan. Even have—*had,* I suppose I must say now—two small pieces from some years back, lucite and ebony. Not much like what you're doing now, of course—or what you *were* doing, should I say? But exquisite, truly beautiful objects. Something of a great, cold sadness about them. I'll not forget them. Though I'll never see them again.

"Like your Cendrars, *je suis l'homme qui n'a plus de passé.* I'm the man with no more past."

Or too much of it, I thought.

I scrabbled in the bag for a beignet. When I bit into it, tatters of steam escaped, and powdered sugar snowed down onto my chest and legs. Outside, the day turned over, turned again, and finally caught.

"It's not at all of any real importance whatsoever that we survive, you know." Planchat savored the last mouthful of coffee and dropped his cup into the waxed-paper bag. "Either the race itself—or you and I individually."

He looked to the window: that quarrel of light.

His eyes, when he turned them to me, were much like the window.

"One of our preservationists observed how difficult it is to recall to our presence that which we've asked to leave. It's just as hard to rid ourselves of what we've summoned. Perhaps more so. All those stories of monsters, deals with diverse devils, three wishes, Gogol's *Nose:* something in our DNA understands all that. Tools aren't readily converted to other use. Axes make poor cuticle scissors."

He walked to the window.

"Do you mind?" Pulling back drapes, opening blinds.

Rivers of light flooded the room.

"There. That's the only speech I have, a short one, and it's done. The story accompanying it will take a bit longer."

He came back across the room and resumed his chair.

"Some months ago I realized I'd come under scrutiny. That I had suddenly become, for some agency or another, whatever its motivation, an object of interest. No single thing I could point up. A half-dozen, then a dozen small, insignificant things. And instinct, of course.

"Once perceived, that interest, that presence, became ever more apparent—finally almost tangible. I couldn't for one moment imagine that it might be other than malignant. And so I fled. Fled *that* life, with its careful, safe architecture, as I'd fled so many others before—and with little more remorse or regret. The quiet years, that interlude, were over. Like Lazarus, I went out into the world again.

"From afar I watched circles of activity around where I'd been, some of it purposeful, much of it puzzling. Eventually I saw that activity withdraw; and what strands I could, I followed. To an electronics lab in Buffalo. To an army base near the Canadian border. Followed the spiraling-down of all these lines, finally, to you.

"Death has sent us a most elaborate invitation, old friend. It occurs to me that we might do well to RSVP that invitation together."

41

We left the hotel together half an hour later by doors opening onto a narrow alley and canyonlike culvert, wearing gabardine overalls liberated from an unwatched laundry and carrying gray plastic bags we'd stuffed with trash.

Quixote at least had his windmills. We didn't know *what* to attack, or where. None of us did.

There was a certain aesthetic to all this, of course, my own motion drawing along these others, their course in turn circumscribed by Planchat; but it was form only, volumes brought to balance, vectors in momentary equilibrium: beautiful speech without intrinsic meaning.

Over beers in an ancient bar just off Canal, still wearing overalls, two workingmen among others, we talked through our options. The nameless bar appeared to be illuminated solely by Dixie Beer signs scattered liberally about. Whenever the street door opened, light started in, then remembered its place and, as though nodding to some unspoken agreement, withdrew. We sat at a high hardwood bar polished smooth as elbows.

It seemed best, we decided, simply for me to continue

what I'd been doing all along: remain visible, stay in the open, wait for storms to come down. As far as we knew, whoever was out there had no idea of Planchat's presence—and that changed the whole equation.

Circles inside circles.

Later we walked down Canal to the river. It was getting towards noon then, people streaming in from every direction to lodge in clusters by fast-food stands and the mouths of restaurants like leukocytes rushing to infection sites. The river was a shining, keen blade of water.

"You cared for your new life?" Planchat said after a while. We'd been sitting quietly, watching as one of the riverboats filled with tourists for its noontime excursion, listening to the steam calliope of another farther down towards skyline and bridge.

"Yes. I did. I learned to."

"And for someone in it?"

"Yes. That, too."

In midwater three barges aligned in a perfect eclipse, then began drawing away from one another.

"She's waiting for you?"

I looked into his face and after a moment said that I didn't know.

Neither of us spoke for several minutes.

"When I realized I was being surveyed," Planchat said, "it was with something very much like relief. I'd passed through a number of careers, at length amassed a considerable personal fortune. Women wandered in and out of my life. I couldn't care for them, didn't feel much of anything, really. Two or three in the morning, I'd find myself deserting my own bed, wishing they weren't there, that I could be again alone. Because I *was* alone,

I'd always been, and these women's bodies beside me, the anxiety and surrender in their eyes, served only to make that fact unbearably painful to me."

Planchat picked up a loose chunk of asphalt and threw it out over the water. A heron tipped towards the ripples it made, then reconsidered.

"I hated it, David. Ten years, and I hated every month, every week, every day, every last moment of it. Now that's all blessedly done with. I'm awake, and the dream is fading. *This* is what I do. Not the only thing I was ever good at, not at all—but the only thing that ever brought me joy."

I knew then that it was Luc, not myself, who would die.

42

THEY CAME IN fast when they came, at four-something the following afternoon, in the tree-shrouded streets just above Tulane, two of them, one in front of me when I turned a corner, the other closing in behind.

No one said anything. I looked from one to the other, instinctively turning sideways. Somehow their concentration wasn't as focused as it should have been, and that didn't make a lot of sense. A little like Doc Holliday stopping off to bird-watch on his way to the O.K. Corral.

Catching an arc of intent that flashed between them, in what amounted to a single motion I looked at A, feinted towards B and came back around in an easy circle to strike at A, who was already moving in to help his partner. The force of my blow, riding on his own momentum, took him down, hard, on his back. And from there it was a simple thing to follow the line of force, feeding it into a body roll that slammed me up against B and dropped him with a loud crack of head against sidewalk.

Frankly, I had no idea that I still had that kind of movement in me.

Education is a wonderful thing.

I looked through their pockets and found the usual half-nothings: faceless keys and a tensor pick, an array of official identification. One wore a suit with Hong Kong's version of an English label and carried British travel papers. The other, in jeans and leather jacket, bore a Polish passport.

That seemed to be all the action. We waited. Finally Planchat stepped out of the cover of trees to join me.

That's life, I was thinking. All the things you wait for, so anticlimactic when they finally happen.

"A disappointing catch, old friend," Planchat said.

Then he looked up—maybe intuition took his gaze there, maybe at that moment (I think he did) he somehow *knew*—at the rooftop of a boarded-up Victorian house nearby.

Silently a black-rimmed hole appeared in his forehead.

I dove for the shelter of the nearest parked car.

One eternity went by strutting.

Then another.

Birdsongs had just started up again when a body came over the roof's side, tumbled through the limbs of a huge pecan tree, and fell motionless to earth.

I waited.

Waited some more, then went over to the body. It had been taken down quite expertly. Garotted, most likely, with a silken cord. Most likely with the silken cord now tied in a bow about the man's genitals.

"Garbage," a voice said beside and above me. "Garbage everywhere. Piled up, tottering, ready to fall. Great stinking bags of it, like this one."

She gestured towards the body there at our feet as I stood.

"Now he can have the eternal hard-on he always wanted. Bastard'll just go on fucking the Void, sticking it in that last dark hole he'll ever sniff at, working away at it forever, while he rots and rots and never comes again."

She smiled.

I remembered a story I'd read in some obscure literary magazine or another. A man is in his psychiatrist's office and the psychiatrist tells him that after exhaustive tests they've found out what's wrong with him. The man awaits this revelation. Well, basically you're crazy as bat shit, the psychiatrist tells him.

I knew her, of course. She was the woman in the vision I'd had in Cross, standing in front of the paintings.

And at our feet was the man with her then, the one whose biography, whose life, I'd acquired afterwards in bits and snatches.

"This really has nothing to do with you," she said. "It was Planchat—Planchat altogether from the start of it. Something from a long time ago, probably now we'll never know what. Not that it could possibly matter."

Her eyes and smile were dark pools where deadly, quiet things lived.

"We all had our borrowed lives. Those careful, makeshift shelters. Then"— she held out, momentarily, a trembling hand—"the web was shaken."

Like a gate springing open, it dropped into my thoughts: *Michael*. The shipbuilder's son, the man who had turned himself into a wolf. *His inquiries had started all this.*

"It was simple for him," she said, nodding to the man at our feet, "to pull the others in. Inevitable that they'd be attracted—so much water rushing to a drain. Like frog legs. Irretrievably dead. But put them in the pot and they go on kicking."

Her mad eyes nudged one last time at the man's body. Then it was as though the body were no longer there. Perhaps not even the memory of it.

"When Planchat felt the circles closing about him and went to ground, his pursuer turned his attentions to you. Thinking this would draw Planchat back into play. Never suspecting, not at first at any rate, that *you'd* already been called back out to pursue *him:* by fleeing, as it turned out. And certainly with no notion—none of you could have had any such intimation—that I was out here as well."

A car came down the street, slowed almost to a stop alongside us, then hurried on. We started away, just another couple out for an afternoon walk beneath the gentle bower of uptown trees. Soon this place would look like an anthill.

I had been more correct than I knew: circles within circles within circles. Michael's high-minded program to complete his father's gratitude spiraling down to the tight curl of unwarranted killings, to flurries of heedless motion, to young Adrian's senseless death on that service road. Metal shavings falling to the floor.

We walked down Freret and across Broadway to St. Charles, to a streetcar stop on neutral ground by the K&B. Tulane and Loyola students in shorts, T-shirts, chinos, polo shirts. Catholic schoolgirls, Amazon-like, pushing the envelope of womanhood in plaid skirts and unpressed white shirts. There my companion looked off into trees bearded with Spanish moss.

"When the hood's taken off," she said, "the hawk has little choice. He's a kind of soft machine, exists only to breed and to kill. And killing is what he does best. Killing's the very reason he lives."

She looked back at me.

"It's been good to see that none of us has lost the fine edge they gave us. You understand that I had to protect you, of course. Because you're my kind. My *only* kind now, I guess."

So she was indeed one of us, with Planchat and myself. Or just myself. The program's rumored third survivor.

"Wait," I said as she stood to leave. The streetcar lumbered camel-like towards us, bucking and swaying. With a shock, with embarrassment, I realized that I still expected, still wanted, it all to *mean* something.

"Johnsson," I said. "Johnsson must have known."

"Yes. Yes, he must have. At some level. If not at first, then surely later on."

It rained all that night in New Orleans. I sat on the balcony of a new hotel in the Quarter picking at scraps of food on my tray, picking at scraps of my life in memory.

Rain obscured the rest of the world and washed over me, and when dawn finally came and I left, it was with a sense that, should I look back, I'd see, abandoned in that chair, my old selves: locust husks clinging to the trees of my childhood.

43

Six days later I was sitting across the table from Gabrielle in a small restaurant in Washington, D.C. From the outside it looked like a fast-lube shop with an awning tacked on; inside, it was replete with healthy plants, waiters in waistcoats and fiftyish men wearing Rolexes in the company of twentyish women wearing red dresses. It was replete also with an appetizer of quail you'd kill for, and with fine, understated continental cuisine, the impression of which had been but slightly diminished by the maître d's response to our wine order: "You bet."

Gabrielle was dissecting a spinach salad with infinite care as I attempted to get down two swallows of coffee before having my cup refilled. Blaise sat by her, knife spreading venison pâté onto bread as though there would never in the history of this earth be any more. I'm not certain, but I think his eyes rolled back each time he took a bite. Then he would sip at his wine, a Brazilian cabernet, and his eyes would roll back again.

Our conversation had been resolutely superficial, as it often is when huge issues loom, all of us tiptoeing about the rims of various abysses. We spoke of wine and food, music, Cendrars, Pavese. Of weather and the way sudden winds come rolling in over New Mexican plains as doors of colored lightning begin opening in the sky.

Over soup, sorbet and salmon, I filled Gabrielle in on what had happened. Events of these past weeks, my personal history insofar as I knew it, the reasons I'd asked her to leave—much as I've written it here. Letting her graft the facts to whatever frame, whatever understanding, she had already. I told her that when first Planchat, and then his pursuer, died, I had died along with them, locked irrevocably to each by those rushes of *otherness* I'd experienced in the past in times of crisis. That, nailed in place, unable even to think or react, I had felt their lives, felt my own, contract to a single gray point, a point that, pulsing, grew ever smaller, smaller, until it was gone—until there was nothing.

Nothing.

Then I looked into her eyes.

"So which has come back to me?" she asked at length. "Creator or killer?"

"Will it frighten you to hear: both?"

"It would frighten me to hear anything else."

To discover what we know, we have only to decide what we will not see. My memories might well be false, but they would, after all, do as well as any others. Every day we reconstruct ourselves out of the salvage of our yesterdays. And a man who has been, even briefly, other men, one who has gone with these men into the shadow—surely he has brought something valuable back from there, surely he must have things to tell us.

I would return to my studio. There I would live for weeks at a time on coffee and hot-plate dinners of stew and soup, and I would produce a stream of sketches, paintings, impressions, life studies, sculptures much like the one long abandoned. Many of these works, these pieces, would be dreamlike. Others would bear into this crowded, wind-torn world an astonishing calm: still places.

Trying to get it right.

Later, all this took on a more reasonable pace, and I emerged from the studio in the evening to music, the smell of a cassoulet I'd put in the oven hours ago, and sometimes friends. And when friends left, when cassoulet, salad and bread were finished, there was always a warm fall night filled with stars and the smell and sounds of life, always a last glass of wine or a final cup of tea, always the moon up there grinning as though it knew the joke. And Gabrielle, always.

About the Author

JAMES SALLIS is a widely accomplished man of letters. His popular Lew Griffin mystery novels—*The Long-Legged Fly, Moth* and *Black Hornet*—have earned nominations for the Edgar and Shamus Awards as well as major critical acclaim. His poetry, essays and short fiction regularly appear in publications ranging from the *Georgia Review* and *Chariton Review* to *The Magazine of Fantasy & Science Fiction* and *Ellery Queen's Mystery Magazine*. *The New Yorker* called his translation of Raymond Queneau's *Saint Glinglin* "so blissfully fizzy that the reader may scarcely notice its complexity." For a time in the 1960s Sallis was editor of the legendary science fiction magazine *New Worlds*. He has published three volumes of musicology and a volume of essays on noir writers. His most recent books include *Ash of Stars: On the Writing of Samuel R. Delany* and *The Guitar in Jazz*. Reviews continue to appear in publications such as *Book World*, *The Bloomsbury Review* and *The Los Angeles Times*. He's written a screenplay, *Big Green*, for a French producer, and recently completed a story commissioned by the BBC. A fourth Lew Griffin novel, *Eye of the Cricket*, will appear this fall.

Past resident of Arkansas, the Midwest, New York, Boston, London, Texas, New Orleans and points between, Sallis currently lives in Phoenix, Arizona, with his wife, Karyn.